AJAY RANE

Global crusader for women's health

Linda

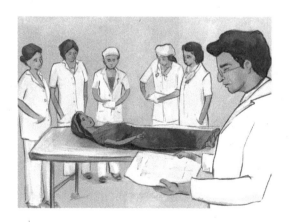

enjoy AJ :)

Aussie
STEM Stars

AJAY RANE
Global crusader for women's health

Story told by DEB FITZPATRICK

WILD
DINGO
PRESS

Aussie STEM Stars series
Published by Wild Dingo Press
Melbourne, Australia
books@wilddingopress.com.au
wilddingopress.com.au

This work was first published by Wild Dingo Press 2022
Text copyright © Deb Fitzpatrick 2022

Cover Design: Gisela Beer
Illustrations: Mirjana Segan
Photo on back cover: Ian Hitchcock
Series Editor: Catherine Lewis
Printed in Australia.
Fitzpatrick, Deb 1972–, author.
Ajay Rane: Global crusader for women's health/Deb Fitzpatrick

 A catalogue record for this
book is available from the
National Library of Australia

ISBN: 9781925893595 (paperback)
ISBN: 9781925893724 (epdf)
ISBN: 9781925893731 (epub)

Family tree

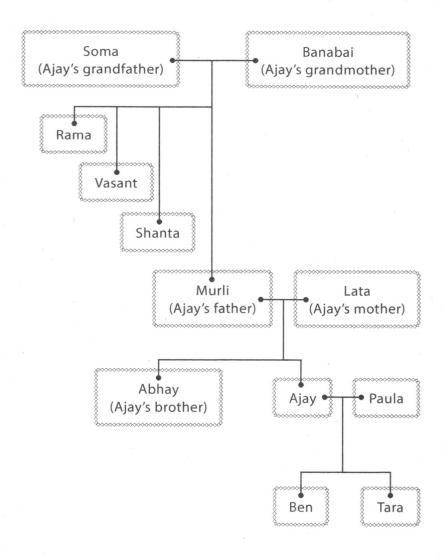

Give 'til it hurts, then you are really giving.
— *Paula Rane*

Contents

Life in the village

There is a saying that goes, 'Behind every great man is a great woman.'

This is the story of Ajay Rane. But in order to understand his story, we need to wind back through history and meet Ajay's father, Murli, and his parents – Ajay's grandparents. For, together, they began a revolution. And Ajay's grandmother, Banabai, is the one who began it all.

*

'Hurry up Murli,' says Banabai, looking out at the stream of villagers heading towards the cotton fields. Some of the children rub their eyes sleepily.

'The others are already on their way. Your father and older brothers left a few minutes ago.'

It is just after six in the morning and the light over the village is soft.

Murli pulls on his leather sandals and slurps down the last of his milky tea. 'Sorry, Aai.' This is what he always calls his mother.

'Here, take some bread to eat on the way or you'll be too hungry to work.'

Murli takes the round, flat **bhakri** from her and presses it, floury and still warm, to his lips. He slings the sack he will fill with cotton in the next few hours over his neck and shoulders. His mother wears a pretty red and orange sari, tied in a special way so she can use some of the fabric as a pouch to store the cotton as she picks. His older sister, Shanta, is dressed similarly.

> **Bhakri** is round, flat unleavened bread often eaten in the state of Maharashtra in India.

Murli, Shanta and their mum slip out of the house and join the quiet procession out to the cotton fields. They pass a rickety wooden shed and Murli spots his father, Soma, and another man repairing one of the farm's bullock carts used to plough the fields.

Soma stops working for a moment, and calls, 'How much are you going to pick today, Murli?'

'Twice as much as yesterday!' Murli replies, grinning.

'Good boy. And then make sure you go to school with the others.'

'Yes Baba.'

'And you must tell me everything you learned tonight.'

'I will.'

'So don't forget anything.'

'No, Baba,' Murli smiled. 'I won't forget a thing.'

*

It's 1943. Murli is 11 years old and lives in the village of Bhalod in Maharashtra in India, with about 800 other villagers.

Banabai and the other women chat as they move into the fields to begin picking at the place where they finished yesterday. The soft white tufts of raw cotton seem to burst from the buds of the plants, like tiny clouds, like a million cotton-wool balls. No one wears gloves, but the pod holding the cotton is sharp, and can easily cut fingers and hands.

Once plucked off, the women throw the raw cotton into the pouches of their saris, or into handmade baskets strapped to their backs.

'Appa!' Murli calls to his friend, beckoning. 'Over here!' It's more fun picking when you have someone beside you. The village kids work in the cotton fields from about the age of nine. The younger ones go out into the fields with their mothers and play, while the babies are wrapped up and put under a shady tree for the day. The young children keep an eye on their siblings.

Picking cotton is hot, hard work. Murli gets tired but knows not to complain because he needs to help his mother, and she *never* complains. Appa stops sometimes and looks towards the green distant hills but doesn't grumble either. He just stares a lot, as if he wishes he were somewhere else.

The hours roll on and the sun gets higher and more intense. Murli tries to ignore how hot he feels by picking the cotton tufts as efficiently as possible, using both hands and filling his sack. He pretends his body is a machine. He's constantly trying to beat his personal best achievement of picking a hundred pounds of cotton in a day. As he picks, he says to himself, almost in time with the picking, *The more I pick, the more money I can give Baba and Aai*. The village record was a massive 300 pounds (136 kg) in a day, and that was picked by one of the fittest, strongest women among the workers.

Finally, Murli hears a call and turns to see Aai and the other women moving towards a large shady area at the edge of the field. He and Appa and the other kids run towards them. This means food!

The women spread bright throws of fabric on the ground and lay out the food. Murli watches as Aai arranges fresh bhakri with her delicious home-made zesty mango pickle and half a raw onion each. He sees that Appa has flatbread too, and onion, but no pickle, which is the best bit. He looks at the generous portions of food Aai has given him.

'Appa,' says Murli. 'I have too much pickle. I can't eat it all. Can you have some for me? Aai will be cross if I waste it.'

Appa's eyes light up. 'I can definitely help you with that problem,' he says, carefully transferring some to his bhakri and taking a mouthful. He groans in appreciation as he chews. 'It is *so good*. Thanks, Murli.'

There is happy chatter all around her, but Banabai is only half-listening. Her youngest son's unstinting kindness and generosity has stolen the show for her yet again. She has seen these selfless acts many times before; it is always others first. Her heart swells and she thanks God for bringing her such a special child.

As they pack up after lunch, Banabai says, 'I will see you after school, Murli.' She softly touches his cheek. 'Look after the others.'

He smiles at her. 'Yes, Aai.' Then he turns to his friend. 'See you tomorrow, Appa. I will tell you all the things Teacher tells us. I will burn them into my memory!'

Appa's father was injured in a farming accident a few years ago, so his family can't afford to send him to primary school. As Murli and the other children begin their one-hour walk to the nearest school, Appa turns back to the cotton field with his mum, where he will work for the rest of the day.

It's about six kilometres to school along the dusty road. The children walk together and laugh as they go. Some of them are only six years old. Murli is among the eldest, at 11. This is his last year at school. Even so, he's one of the lucky ones, unlike Appa. Next year Murli, too, will have to work full-time on the farm, like his brothers and sister.

Only children from the higher **castes** will continue their education at high school. And there are no children like that in his village. In Bhalod there are only lower caste, poor families. That's why they work in the cotton fields. None of the children in the village of Bhalod will go to high school, they all know that.

The **caste system** decides a person's place in Indian society. It is an age-old system that Indians are born into. Caste is determined by wealth, occupation, and family background. In 1955 a law was passed in India making discrimination based on caste illegal. However, it still occurs.

On their way home, Murli and some of the other children stop to gather sticks for cooking fires. They tuck them under their arms. With so many people in the village, any twigs and branches on the ground are quickly stockpiled. The village women also collect sticks for home fires during the day, and to make them go further, cooking fires are often shared between several houses.

That night the Rane family shares dinner of bread, **dal** and delicious potatoes cooked with curry leaves and black mustard seeds, all cooked over the open fire and eaten adeptly with their fingers. Murli's legs are tired from the trek to school and back, but his mind is not tired. It is full and bouncing with the many things he learned in the classroom that afternoon.

'Did you know,' he says between mouthfuls of creamy dal, 'that India has an active volcano?'

Dal is a dish of lentils and is a staple of Indian cooking.

Before anyone can respond, he says, 'It's in the Andaman and Nicobar Islands'.

'Where are they?' Banabai asks. 'That doesn't sound like India.'

'They're way down near Indonesia, but now India owns them. There are hundreds of islands in the group.

'*And*,' Murli goes on, eyes wide, 'the Andaman Islands are home to *an uncontacted tribe* called the ... Sentina ... Sentinelese, I think is how you say it.'

Soma chuckles. 'Hard to pronounce.'

'Can you imagine being in a group of people no one has *ever* made contact with?'

'Sounds idyllic,' Banabai says, beginning to clear the dishes.

Murli and the others stand and help their mum clean up. Soma puts more sticks on the fire to boil water for chai tea, which he will make with black tea leaves, milk and spices.

As they sip their tea his father calls him.

'Murli, come!'

Murli trots to his side.

'What is it, Baba?'

Soma prods a piece of paper.

'That – what does that say?'

Murli often has to help his parents read things. His father only had a few years' schooling, and his mum is **illiterate**, like most people

> If you are **illiterate** you are unable to read and write.

in the village. The wealthier farm owners aren't; they are from higher castes and have been to school.

Banabai nods as Murli reads out the trickier words to his father.

'That's it, Murli,' she says in her quiet voice. 'You keep studying at school. Learn everything.'

She looks at Soma, and says, 'The only path to improvement is via education'.

He nods, murmurs his agreement. They have been talking about this a lot recently.

But unlike Australia, where attending school is compulsory to the age of 17, in India and many other developing countries, education is a privilege, not a right, with only the wealthy able to access secondary schooling and beyond.

2

The special one

Murli hears them at night when he has gone to bed – Aai and Baba, talking quietly, Aai speaking more than usual, and with an urgency in her voice. He gets out of the bed he shares with his brother to eavesdrop one night, but Vasant calls him back.

'I want to know what they're talking about,' Murli says.

'If they're whispering it's a sign they don't want us to know.'

'Exactly!' Murli explains, but reluctantly obeys his brother. He lies there, unable to sleep, straining to hear his parents' conversation over Vasant's growing snore.

The next night a community meeting is to be held. Murli always loves these nights. They only happen occasionally but are like a big village party, with everyone staying up later than usual. The women put down mats where families sit and eat, sharing food and stories from the day's work in the fields. Some people huddle in private conversation and there is always plenty of giggling and teasing, especially among the kids and teenagers.

Murli and Appa's families sit together with three others, and Murli watches in delight as Aai reveals a dish of **okra**, his all-time favourite vegetable. The fact that it looks like little hairy torpedoes, or big chillies, is just a bonus.

Okra is a fuzzy green vegetable that can be fried, roasted or added to stews or curries. It's grown all over the world and is highly nutritious. Okra is sometimes called 'ladies' fingers'.

When all the food is gone, some of the village's leaders stand to speak. There is news about one of the villagers who has been very sick. He'd been vomiting for several days, and then had a seizure. His family pushed him by **oxcart** to the nearest medical clinic, two villages away.

An **oxcart** is a wooden cart pulled by an ox. Oxcarts were the main mode of transport in India for many years and are still used today. They are sometimes called bullock carts. (It's one ox but two oxen, by the way.)

Pesticide is a poison used to kill pests and is commonly used in agriculture.

Nakul says, 'The doctor thinks Sakash has suffered a reaction to the **pesticide** spray used on the crop last week. I spoke to the landowners this morning but they said that's rubbish, that it's harmless. I'm not sure they have our best interests at heart. We must be careful.'

'The landowners need to tell us when they are going to use it,' a man calls out, 'so we can stay away from the fields for a few hours.'

People murmur their agreement.

'Otherwise, more of us will get sick.'

'And that will be bad for business,' says another.

'And terrible for our families,' says someone else.

14

'They have to take responsibility!' A young man cries out.

The community nods as one.

'Prayers for Sakash,' Nakul says, and heads drop as the villagers pray silently.

There is a pause. A bat swoops to catch a moth, and is gone as quickly as it came. Then Murli sees Baba stand up and move to the front of the group. He clears his throat.

'This matter with Sakash reminds us that we need to take care of ourselves. And that begins with our children,' he says. His voice is positive and gentle.

'Banabai and I have been talking. We have been thinking about the children of this village. All of us work here on the cotton plantation all our lives for a few coins each day. We have barely enough to feed and clothe ourselves. Some of us are lucky enough to be able to send our children to primary school; that is something,' says Soma.

'But none of us – not one – can afford to send even one of our children to high school. So they will spend their lives working here also, whether they want to or not. And *their* children will work here, and theirs after that. Long hours, doing menial, repetitive, dirty work, year in, year out.'

People nod grimly.

'It's a cycle,' Soma says. 'A trap we can't get out of. And we're condemning any child we bring into this world to the same life. The only ones improving themselves are the landowners; they are getting richer on our backs.'

Murli looks around him. Everyone is staring at his father, hanging on his every word. *Baba is a leader*, Murli thinks. *People listen to him, look up to him.* Pride fills his chest.

Soma continues: 'Banabai and I have been contemplating an idea. We humbly ask you to listen and consider it.'

Murli turns and looks at Aai. Her eyes are shining, locked on Baba.

'We accept that, as families, we cannot afford to send our children to secondary school. But what if we put the little that we have together? We could do something with that.

'Last night, Banabai said to me, "If we each put a copper coin into a pot at the end of every day, we might be able to save enough for one child to continue their education".'

Soma goes on, 'Bhalod's children are as intelligent and curious as any children anywhere. That we, their parents, are poor is not their fault. Let us work together so at least one of them can break out of poverty.'

'But how much do we need to make this happen?' someone calls out.

'A copper coin – just whatever you can manage – when the farmer gives us our wages. After a year, if all of us contribute just a little, we should have enough. It doesn't matter if one gives less and one gives more. It will all go into the pot and will add up.'

Smoke from cooling fires moves around them. Murli scans the crowd. People are looking at one another, eyebrows raised in interest at the idea.

'One special child from the village, chosen by us all, in agreement. We could be advised by the schoolteacher to help us make the right choice.'

'And what about those left behind?' a man asks. 'What for them?'

'You are right,' Soma sighs. 'It is not fair. Nothing about the caste system in this country is fair.' It makes his blood boil, but he does not say that.

'But it's impossible to raise the funds to send every one of these deserving children to school, we must accept that.'

Murli walks home with his brothers and sister, carefully carrying the leftovers of dinner. His brothers talk animatedly about the meeting. There is something new that Murli feels all around him. It's a gentle, good feeling that goes deep.

'What do you think of what Baba said, Shanta?'

She looks across at him, and Murli sees she is sad.

'I think it is good, little brother,' she says.

He waits. An ox lows mournfully in the distance.

'But it won't be a girl who goes. It won't change anything for us.'

Murli's heart misses a beat. He wants to say *That's not true!* but he knows she is right. Many girls in the village do not even get primary schooling. If money is short, the girls are first to miss out.

Though it isn't openly talked about, Murli understands that girls are considered less valuable than boys. Women's status is very low. They never speak at meetings, for example; only the men do.

In the dark, he reaches out and puts his hand in Shanta's. She squeezes.

'It's okay, little brother. It's just life.'

The moon is high. It's late and Murli is overcome with tiredness.

*

The next few months tick over like all the others before. The villagers of Bhalod work hard every day for their handful of coins. They laugh as they go, and they care for one another like members of one big family. Their hands get scratched and their backs ache. As they leave the cotton fields, with the sun melting behind the hills, they drop a coin, maybe two, into an earthenware pot Banabai has left out.

At first a few copper coins sprinkle the bottom of the pot, but after a month or so, the clay bottom can no longer be seen. By the time the rains come in June, the pot is one-third full. The coins are mainly annas – one sixteenth of a **rupee** – but there are a few quarter rupees in there too.

> The **rupee** is the name of Indian money (like our dollar).

The months slip by and the pot becomes so heavy it can no longer be moved.

Professor Sir Ajay Rane PSM OAM

MBBS Msc MD FRCS FRCOG FRANZCOG
CU FICOG(Hon) Phd FRCPI(Hon) FACOG, GAICD
Head & Chair of Obstetrics & Gynaecology
College of Medicine & Dentistry
Medicine, Health & Molecular Science

T. +61 47663699 (Ph) +61 47663696(Fax)
E ajay.rane@jcu.edu.au W jcu.edu.au
Townsville campus townsville QLD 4811 Australia

CRICOS Provider Code 00117J

JAMES COOK
UNIVERSITY
AUSTRALIA

Cairns
Singapore
Townsville

Soma's whispered night-time conversations begin again.

'Teacher says he is the most inquisitive and the most diligent,' Murli hears Baba say one night.

'But we can't suggest he be the one – the others will think that was what we planned all along, and it isn't!' Aai says.

'Murli,' Vasant hisses from the bed. 'Come back to bed.'

Murli puts his fingers to his mouth, silently pleading, *Shhh!* He peers around the fabric that acts as a door between the rooms.

'We must let the villagers choose,' Aai insists. 'The process must be fair. I don't want to have anything to do with the final decision.'

Baba nods. 'It must be fair, yes. And everyone must have a say.'

Aai is quiet, then speaks softly. 'Many people say things, though. About Murli.'

'Yes, I hear things too,' says Baba. Through the tiny crack, Murli sees Baba takes his mother's hands and they sit like this for a moment. Baba sighs. 'What is right will happen.'

Aai nods.

*

It is the night of the village meeting. There has been chatter all day about the food being cooked and what will be discussed. Earlier in the week, the children had been excited to see some of the village men arrive at school. The teacher had left the classroom for what felt like an age to speak with them.

'Carry on with practising the spelling words, children,' she had said as she left. 'Conscious, infectious, spacious, superstitious, vicious … and keep going down the list right to the end. Write each word three times. Then you may test one another.'

None of the children wrote a thing; they were too busy rubbernecking out the window at the adults.

'Teacher is talking about us!' Guneet exclaimed.

'What is she saying?!'

'Something about reading levels,' Guneet replied. 'And eagerness. And … logic.'

Then turning suddenly, he lowered his voice, 'Shhh, they're coming!'

The children scrambled and the classroom miraculously returned to its normal studiousness.

'Well,' said Teacher, clearly delighted as she came back in, the adults poking their heads through the door. 'Well done, children.'

She passed the men a file from her drawer, with the school stamp on the front.

'Please take your time to look at these records. It might help. Though I stand by my recommendation.'

*

Murli and his siblings help to carry plates of food to the meeting place. Everyone sits in small and large groups eating and chatting before the formalities begin. Once they've finished their potatoes and bhakri, Murli and Appa play marbles on the ground while their parents talk.

Finally, one of the older men stands.

'As you know, we have all been contributing what we can to the education fund. We thank Soma and Banabai for this plan to help one lucky child. It is a way forward for an individual, but also for our village.'

There is general agreement from the crowd.

'We have all had time now to speak with one another about who might be given this scholarship, and several of us met with the schoolteacher this week. In every conversation, one name came up. Other children were mentioned too, but none as often as this child. Which is why the decision has been almost made for us, thank God.'

Murli can barely breathe. All the children wait, faces shining up at the man speaking.

'We are so proud and happy to offer this special opportunity to you ... Murli Rane.'

Murli hears his mother breathe in sharply. Then she grabs him.

'Oh! Murli! Oh! Go, go to the front.' She pushes him gently.

Vasant stands up, eyes full. He beams at his little brother.

'Well done, Murli!'

As he makes his way to the front as if in a dream, his friends leap and jump all around him. 'Murli, Murli!' they cry happily.

And Appa. Appa is there, his arm around his friend's shoulders. 'Murli,' he says, 'this is it. This is your chance – fly!'

3

The long road

It's a long bus ride to the high school but Murli tries to savour every moment, knowing how hard all the other kids of Bhalod, including his brothers and sister, are working on the cotton farm. He couldn't sleep last night for being so excited, then thoughts about how unfair it is that only one child can go wormed their way around his mind like maggots in a guava. And, finally, there was the matter of: *Am I good enough?*

After an hour of his tossing and turning, Vasant sighed and said, 'What is it, Murli? What's the matter?'

When Murli explained, his brother said, 'Please don't worry. It's not your fault more children from the village can't go.' He paused. 'Think of it this way. What you learn, you can teach us. Dinner time will be so much more interesting now, with your news from the world beyond Bhalod.'

Murli swiped away a tear, rolled towards his brother and whispered, 'Thank you'. He felt so lucky to be part of this family. Then he slid away into sleep.

*

It's his bag that gives him away. All the others have smart satchels, but Murli has a hand-sewn cotton bag over his shoulder. A couple of the boys stand together with their shiny shoes and look scornfully at him.

Murli pretends to ignore them and looks around the classroom. There are three girls in the room of about 20 students. None of the children – not one – is from his caste. He feels shame in a way he never has before.

And then the teacher strides in and everyone stands stock-still until the man before them smiles warmly and says, 'Please be seated'.

Over the next five years, Murli devours everything taught to him. What fascinates him most is science, particularly human biology. Learning how the body works and what a clever organism it is focuses his attention like nothing else. In his final two years at high school, with the encouragement of his teacher, Murli determines to devote his life to the scientific marvel of the human body.

'Baba, Aai,' he says one evening, over a huge portion of bhakri and vegetables, 'I think I've decided what I want to do at university'.

Everybody stops chewing and looks at him.

Aai's eyes light up. Witnessing her youngest child's education has been a joy to her. Though she sorely misses his company in the fields, she fills the lonely moments with thoughts of what he might be learning at school.

'And what is that, Murli?' Baba asks quietly. 'What do you want to study?'

'You'd better not say you want to be a farmer, little brother,' Vasant says, grinning.

Murli laughs. 'No risk of that.' He takes a breath. 'I know it's a lot of work, and I still have to get the marks, but...'

'Your marks have been outstanding, son,' Baba says. 'Every year.'

'Well, they may not be good enough for medicine.'

'Medicine?' Aai whispers. 'Medicine? You want to be a doctor?'

Murli blushes. 'Yes, Aai, if I can.'

She stares at him. A thousand feelings pass through her. 'You can, Murli.' She gets up and pulls him up too. 'You can, Murli, I know you can!' she exclaims, dancing with him in the tiny house while tears roll down her face.

*

Two years later, the letter from Mumbai arrives.

Dear Master Murli Rane,
Re: Letter of Offer

I am delighted to offer you entry into the 1949 Pre-medical Programme at Elphinstone College. Congratulations on achieving entry into this highly competitive programme, which, on successful completion, will grant you entry to medical degree programmes at India's best medical schools.

We look forward to welcoming you to our campus.

Yours sincerely,
Arjun Patel
Vice-Chancellor
Elphinstone College

There is a great deal more dancing in the Rane household, and a village celebration is held the night before Murli departs for the big, far away city of Mumbai. Aai cooks all his favourite dishes, including a double batch of okra. She is generous with her spices and uses twice as much **ghee** as normal to make delicious buttery, garlicky bhakri.

Ghee
Butter oil made by heating butter on a low heat for 15 minutes until the water in it evaporates and the milk solids can be removed. It originated in ancient India and is used in cooking.

After the feast, Murli stands shyly to speak.

'I would not be going to university if it weren't for all of you. I can never thank you enough. I hope I live up to your expectations.'

He turns to Soma and Banabai.

'Baba and Aai ... thank you for giving up so much for me. Thank you for having the idea all those years ago to make this possible. And thank you for your wonderful cooking. I might get very hungry in the city.'

He falls quiet and looks at all the smiling faces around him.

'I will miss you all so much.'

The rest of the evening is spent in a whirl of hugs and love.

The following day, 17-year-old Murli leaves for Mumbai to begin university. The city is 400 kilometres from Bhalod. As the bus makes its way along the dusty road, hands fly up into the air from the cotton fields and farm sheds and shouts of good wishes float towards him. Murli leans out the open window and waves with both arms. Then he sits down and looks at the road ahead. He's completely alone. Medical school? Who on earth does he think he is?

His amazement is shared by others: the phenomenon of a poor student from Bhalod attending university is such an oddity that it makes front-page news in the 4 September 1949 edition of *The Weekly of India*. The photo of Murli on the train to Mumbai – the first time he'd been on a train – shows a grinning young man embarking on a brave new adventure.

Everything at Elphinstone goes brilliantly. Murli studies hard, completes his pre-medical course and then gains entrance to Mumbai's Grant Medical College to do his medical degree. By now Murli is used to life in the massive city and has even learned to cook, though he hankers for Aai's meals. His only trips home are during semester breaks, but he makes the most of these, laughing with his siblings and regaling everyone with stories of life in the 'big smoke'. He helps Baba fix farm equipment as Murli is now too old to work in the fields with the women and children.

But leaving is always so hard.

*

'Nurse, can you help me with this, please?' Murli enquires, head poking into the bustling hospital corridor. Now 25 and an intern in the Emergency Department, it is his job to attend to patients with all kinds of medical problems.

'Yes, Doctor?'

'We need to give this patient more pain relief, please.' He checks the patient's file at the end of his bed. 'He's experiencing chest pain. A second dose of the medication he was given on arrival should make him much more comfortable.'

'I'll do so right away, Doctor.'

Murli looks at her. It's hard not to notice her unusual green eyes. He sees her name badge.

'Thank you, Nurse Lata.'

That week, he and Nurse Lata seem to have the same roster – including long night shifts which Murli is still getting used to. They work well together, and he starts to seek her out whenever he needs assistance.

One evening, as they complete some paperwork at the nurses' station, Murli makes sure no one else is around before saying, 'Nurse Lata, I know a place that makes a very good **biriyani**. Could I request the pleasure of your company when I go there tomorrow for dinner?'

Biriyani is an Indian dish of seasoned rice with meat, fish or vegetables.

Much lighter skinned than Murli, Nurse Lata's blush is instant and undeniable.

'Oh!' She smiles. 'Well.' She puts her pen down. 'Well…'

Murli adds, 'It's just in Mahim. It would be an easy stroll from here.'

'Well, then,' Lata says, 'that sounds very nice, thank you. I would like to.'

Murli tries to keep his grin under control, but he is chuffed. *She is gorgeous*, he thinks. *Smart and kind.*

'Shall we say straight after our shift, then?'

Murli and Lata fall in love, like two leaves falling from a tree, spinning towards one another. They share many interests and care about the same things. He admires the fact that as well as the long hours she works in the hospital, she finds the time and energy to volunteer at a local charity.

However, what they do not share is the same status in India's social system. Despite now being a doctor, Murli is still judged by the reputation of the poor caste he was born into. Lata is from a much higher caste. She is also light-skinned; he is very dark. None of the parents, not even Baba and Aai, are happy about their relationship.

But Murli and Lata are in love! And love breaks down all barriers ... doesn't it?

Murli visits his family in the hope he will receive their blessing. It's a very difficult visit.

'But you have met her! You must agree she is a perfect match for me, Baba.'

'I don't agree. She is a non-vegetarian for one thing.'

Murli tilts his head to one side. 'Oh, Baba. And the other things?'

Soma closes his eyes for a moment, as if to begin the conversation again.

'She *is* very nice, yes, son, but the problems of being from such different castes will never leave you.'

'I do not accept that,' Murli says. 'If it's one thing I've learned from you and Aai – from what you did for me by funding my education – it's that what you are born into is *not* who you are. You taught me that, Baba!'

'I will not discuss it any further.'

'I am very sorry,' Murli says. 'I have always wanted to do the right thing by you. But this… This is right. For me.' He breathes out slowly. 'Also, I've been offered a place at a university in England to study for my surgery qualification.'

Aai smiles with pride, but says sadly, 'We will never see you'.

'Yes, you will,' Murli replies gently. 'I've been offered a good job there, so I'll be able to come back each year.'

He hugs them both, long and hard, and, with stinging tears, leaves Bhalod.

When he arrives in Mumbai, Lata is waiting. Their belongings are packed. They begin their life together.

*

Happily settled in England, in 1962 two very important things happen for Murli and Lata. Murli becomes a Fellow of the Royal College of Surgeons, a qualification that means he can work as a surgeon anywhere in the world. But even more joyfully, their second son is born, making the little family complete. Ajay joins his three-year-old brother Abhay, and life is full.

In his new role as a surgeon, Murli is able to give his children an excellent education – something that he nearly missed out on. They also enjoy a luxury he could only dream of as a child: a car. Life in England is very comfortable. Murli's career is going gangbusters and, when he's not working, he loves spending time with their two boys.

'Snow!' He hears the excited squeal. 'Daddy, it's snowed in the night!' Ajay says.

'Isn't it beautiful!'

'Can we make a snowman?'

'Yes, yes!!' Abhay chimes in. 'We need a carrot for the nose. Mummy, do we have any carrots?'

Lata reaches into their modern fridge and finds a bag of carrots. She pulls out a huge, pointy one.

'This should do it,' she says, holding it like a sword. 'Look, it's even got a nasty long hair coming out of it, just like an old man's nose would have!'

Ajay and Abhay pull on their boots and mittens and go out into the bright white world. Ajay jumps up and down and falls over, sinking into the soft powder. Abhay gathers handfuls of snow and packs it into a perfect ball, aims, and fires it at his brother. It explodes off his shoulder and the game is on!

Murli smiles, watching them through the window. Everything is perfect.

So why does he feel troubled? Why does he feel as though something is missing?

'Do you think about home much?' he asks Lata.

'Yes, of course.'

'Life is very good here, isn't it?'

'Yes,' she says. 'We want for nothing.'

'Yes, exactly,' Murli says.

'What do you mean?' Lata looks confused.

'It's too good,' he says.

'*Too* good?'

'Think about all those people in Bhalod who made this possible – this life for us. It would never have been like this without them.'

'That's true, Murli, but they are happy for your success and you're always very generous when you go home.'

'It's not just the money. It's their quality of life, their access to some of the things we consider to be basic services – medical services, I mean.'

Lata is very still. She knows what is coming.

'What are you saying?' she asks.

'I want to give back,' Murli says, voice cracking. 'To them. The community that made my journey possible. They deserve something back from me. I can't forget the people who have made me who I am.'

4

Not life as we know it

Ajay can't believe how lucky he is, travelling on a huge passenger ship to exotic India! What an adventure! He pinches himself as he walks with his family along the promenade deck, looking out over the vast ocean. At night he falls asleep to the gentle lulling movement of swells beneath the vessel.

His mum is quiet while Daddy talks to them about growing up in India, and how they'll be staying in the same village as Grandmother and Grandfather.

'How long will we be in India, Daddy?'

Murli looks quickly at Lata and says, 'Well, a year initially and then we'll see how things go. I would like to help as many people as I can. There are many, many people living in India, Ajay, as you will see — many more than in England — but not enough surgeons to help them all.'

'Will you do operations on them, Daddy?' Ajay asks.

Murli laughs.

'Well, only if they need one!'

One night not long before the ship is due to arrive in Mumbai, Ajay is sure he hears his mother weeping into her pillow.

As the boat docks at the port, Ajay and his brother scan the new world before them. The port is smelly and dirty and busy. In fact, Ajay has never ever seen so many people in one spot. Men wearing what look like skirts shout and direct oxcarts. Some have turbans on their heads. Women wear long, colourful saris

A **sari** is a long piece of cotton or silk, the main outer garment of Hindu women, worn round the body with one end over the head or shoulder.

like his grandmother's and some have scarves covering their hair. Children walk around, many in bare feet. There are immigration officials and policemen in uniforms. There are bicycles and oxcarts everywhere, crossing in every direction. Road rules don't seem to apply here. It is mad.

Abhay claps his hand over his nose.

'What is that smell?' he hisses.

Daddy nods.

'It's the smell of an impoverished, over-populated country, Abhay. It's not nice, is it.'

Mummy is frantically waving a fan across her face. Beads of sweat have burst onto her skin.

'The heat,' she says. 'I'd forgotten.'

Ajay moves closer to her, and looks out at the strangeness around him. This isn't exotic in the way he'd imagined.

His eyes watch the footpath below. There are people lying there, right in the way of pedestrians. A few of them line the concrete path in a row. Next to them huddles a whole family. And there's a boy about Ajay's age sitting on a piece of cardboard, looking up at the ship. The two boys' eyes meet momentarily.

Overwhelmed by the smells, noise and pressing heat, Ajay and his brother fall asleep in the taxi to the village. It's hours later when Ajay wakes up. He smells woodsmoke and hears the murmur of voices in the next room. He looks around. Abhay must already be up. He leaps off his bed, which is an old mattress on the floor, and follows the voices.

'Aaji!' he squeals, rushing into the folds of his grandmother's green sari.

Banabai reaches down and picks him up, joy on her face.

'Look how you have grown! You have stretched like an elastic band, young Aju. How handsome you are. It is so good to see you!' She touches his face with her gentle open palm.

'Where is Grandpa?…ahh, Aajoba, I mean,' asks Ajay.

'He's at work but will be home for a special lunch to celebrate this wonderful day,' Aaji says.

Right then they hear a scream, and a door slam.

Abhay bolts inside, his eyes pulled wide like pool balls.

'What?' Mummy says. 'What is it?'

'The—'

They wait. His face is grey.

'Abhay, what is it, my darling?' Mummy asks.

'The toilet,' he says. 'There's—'

'There's what?' Ajay asks.

Abhay turns to him. 'There's...a pig in it.'

'What do you mean?! A live pig?'

'Yes, *a live pig*!'

'In the toilet? In the bowl?'

Abhay shakes his head. 'No, not *in* the bowl. There is no bowl. There's just a hole underneath where you sit. A sort of *pit*.'

'So where's the pig?' asks a now terrified Ajay.

'In the pit,' Abhay whispers. '*Under your bum*.'

Ajay shakes his head. This cannot be true. He can't imagine it and tries not to, because soon he'll need to go and he already really, *really* doesn't want to.

'And it *stinks*,' Abhay says. 'And there are flies all around you, landing on you – they're everywhere.'

'Ahh.' Mummy sits down at the table and indicates for the boys to sit too. She reaches out for their hands. Aaji disappears into another part of the house.

'Boys, life here in India is very different from the life we've been used to. We've enjoyed so much comfort in England – everything is clean, everything is easy. But that's not how many people in the world live,' she says.

'The toilets here are different. The way things are dealt with here are different. Fresh water doesn't just come out of every tap,' she says.

She points. 'See those buckets?'

Ajay nods. There were two buckets full to the brim with water.

'Here, water is precious. That water has been carried from the village well. It's only for drinking and cooking with. It's far too precious to waste down the loo. Most people in India don't have flushing toilets. And many in rural areas like this have ... a pig ... to deal with things.'

Ajay swallows.

Mummy squeezes their hands.

'I'll show you how to use the loo so it's not scary.'

'I'm not using it,' says Abhay. 'Ever!'

'It's a lot to get used to, I know,' says Mummy.

'I don't want to get used to it!' Abhay explodes. 'I'll never get used to it – I hate it! Why are we even here? Why did we come? What was wrong with England? I want my friends, my school, *my toilet*!!'

Mummy gets up. Her face is grim.

'I know. It's hard,' she says. She takes a breath. 'But your father's work is vital. He wants to help people no one else will help. The world has forgotten these people. And if we support Daddy, then we too are helping these forgotten people in a way.'

Ajay knows this is an important conversation, but his mind is stuck on something else: the live pig in the toilet. And how he might not go for a while yet.

When he does go in, he takes Daddy with him. Murli explains how the system works.

'It's so efficient,' he says. 'And does not use a drop of water. I think it's what you call a win-win situation, Ajay.'

Abhay hangs on for three days. During that time he searches the village for other options – a public toilet? (none exist) or a well-located tree or bush (but there are always people about. There are people *everywhere you turn*.) Finally, Abhay can wait no longer. When he comes out of the pig loo, his face is streaked with tears. He doesn't speak to anyone for some time.

*

Once the Ranes have settled in a bit and their dad has found work at a local hospital, it's time for Ajay and Abhay to start school. The nearest school that teaches in English is 25 kilometres away from the village. The brothers will have to catch a public bus there each day — very different from the short walk they took to school with their mum back in England. Ajay is only seven years old. He tries to imagine himself on a bus without either of his parents and isn't at all sure he likes the idea. If it weren't for his big brother, he would be very worried indeed. Neither of them speaks Marathi, the local language, other than a few basic words of greeting and thanks.

The boys wake just after five o'clock so they are ready for the six o'clock bus. It's still dark as the bus groans away from the village, and when the sky lightens, Ajay sees the silhouettes of chickens, goats, and cows.

As the bus trundles along he looks out at the landscape that couldn't be more different from the green smooth curves of England which Ajay fondly remembers from the family's many weekend drives into the country. Nor are there red

A 'bobby' is a slang word for a police officer in England.

double-decker buses here, or '**bobbies**' directing traffic. Instead, there are dilapidated old buses lurching over potholed roads and a cacophony of horns being tooted by every moving vehicle.

One morning the boys are sleepy and only realise half an hour into their journey that the bus is going in the wrong direction.

'Abhay, where are we?' Ajay asks, staring out the glassless window. 'I don't recognise this.'

Abhay looks around, confused.

'I don't know ... did you see the bridge?'

The bridge is the landmark the boys watch for each morning, and once they see it they know they are safely on their way to school.

'No, I didn't. We have to get off and go back!'

'Driver, stop please!' Abhay calls, standing up, slinging his schoolbag over his shoulder.

The bus grinds to a halt and the boys stand in a cloud of dust from the unsealed road.

'We have to catch a bus back,' says Ajay.

They cross the road and wait for five, ten, then 15 minutes.

'Teacher will be ringing the bell soon,' Ajay says, hopping from foot to foot.

Abhay peers up the road. Truck after truck passes them, each adding to the boys' now very dusty hair. Abhay sticks his arm out and yells something toa man hanging off the back of a truck trundling towards them. The man calls to the driver to slow down and hurries the boys onto the tray. There are benches around the three sides which are all full of people. Others squat in the centre area. One woman is carrying two chickens in a round cane cage. The boys squeeze in and the man yells again to the driver to continue.

Ajay looks at his older brother in awe.

'How did you do that? You're a genius!' he exclaims.

Abhay shrugs. He's not sure how he pulled it off but is very relieved to be heading in the right direction. After all, his parents told him that, as the older brother, he's in charge.

They see the bridge, get off the truck and wait two minutes for the right bus. Abhay sits a little taller in his chair at school that day. Maybe things won't be so bad after all.

One night, over a meal of dal and a slimy chilli-shaped vegetable called okra that the boys don't enjoy anywhere near as much as their parents do, Grandmother and Grandfather tell them

> The word **Diwali** literally means 'row of lights' in the ancient Indian language, Sanskrit.

about **Diwali**. It's a special celebration coming up; a festival. Most Indians – in India and in other countries – celebrate it each year.

'Diwali is the Festival of Lights, boys,' Aajoba says. 'It's one of the most important religious festivals for **Hindus** and **Sikhs**.'

> **Hindus**: follow Hinduism, the main religion in India.
> **Sikhs**: follow Sikhism, a religion founded in India in the 16th century.

'What happens?' Ajay asks, dropping a blob of dal on his leg. He's still mastering eating with his hands.

'We have five days of celebrating, eating delicious foods, lighting candles and giving thanks,' Aaji says. 'People clean their homes and decorate them with lights and oil lamps called "diyas". There are gifts and sweets, and people wear new clothes.'

'There are fireworks,' chips in Daddy.

The boys look at each other. Ajay can't wipe the grin off his face.

'When does it start?' he cries.

The next day after school, Mummy comes home from a shopping mission and opens a bag. Inside, Ajay sees a pair of the latest-fashion bell-bottom pants. His eyes widen. *Could they be...?*

'Yes, Ajay, they're for you,' Mummy says, smiling. 'Try them on! Go on, take them. Do you like the colour?'

Ajay holds up the pants. He nods. They are magnificent. He races to the room he shares with Abhay and pulls them on. They fit beautifully and make him look so ... cool!

He *loves* Diwali already!

'I have a new shirt for you, Abhay,' Mummy calls. 'And some new shoes for me,' she says happily.

Over the next few days they set up what seems like a million tealights inside and outside their house. This is done in every home, and at night, when they are lit, the whole village twinkles happily.

'The lights and lamps are said to help the Hindu goddess of wealth, Lakshmi, find her way into people's homes,' his mum explains as they arrange the little candles. 'She brings prosperity.'

Ajay smells cooking from every house and at night they gather in big groups to eat crispy, spicy samosas, sticky gulab jamun, and pakora. Yum! There are round patties called aloo tikki and bowls of crunchy chivda to snack on. It is a feast of flavours and treats, with many sweet dessert recipes saved just the festival. Ajay is sure his bell bottoms are fitting tighter around his waist by the end of the festivities.

On the last night, they watch colourful fireworks spray-paint the sky. Ajay hears his grandfather murmuring his thanks for everything from the cows in the field to Daddy's surgical instruments to the cooking pots in the kitchen. Nothing is too ordinary to be worshipped.

I worship the fireworks, Ajay thinks, lying in bed that night. *And my bell bottoms. And my family.* And then he falls asleep.

5

Gowning up
with Daddy

Because school starts early, it finishes early, and the
boys are usually home by early afternoon. They
have a cooked lunch and for Ajay the highlight
is his grandmother's homemade pickles – mango
kasundi, vegetable achaar, and lime pickle. Even
thinking about them makes his mouth water.

'Have some more pickle,' Aaji leans over and
whispers to him. 'I made extra for you and your
dad.'

Ajay and Abhay have jobs they do after school before they can relax and play games together or read. Abhay has to bring two buckets of water from the well and Ajay helps Kamala, the home help, wash the pots and pans after cooking. While they work, Kamala tells him stories that have been passed down from generation to generation for centuries.

He loves listening to these tales of Hindu gods and goddesses, divine feats, tyranny, treachery, bravery and sacrifice. Stories of boys being eaten by evil eagles and tales of beautiful forests becoming dark-hearted. There were stories of wicked snakes and of fierce warrior goddesses. Every day over the dirty dishes Kamala shares a new story with him. Ajay has never been so keen to do the washing up!

*

'Boys, Mummy and I have some exciting news. We're moving to a new house,' Daddy says. 'It's two-storey, and it won't just be a house for us to live in, but a hospital. A new hospital for the people who live around here.'

On the day of the move, Ajay packs all of his things into big sacks. Daddy arranges for a man to drive their sacks and suitcases to the new house. Aaji and Aajoba give them huge hugs.

'But we'll see you very soon, Aaji,' says Ajay. 'Daddy says the new house is only a short bus ride away.'

'Yes,' she says. 'We are excited to see your new home! You will need some jars of pickle, won't you?'

Ajay nods. Nothing will taste the same without it. He suddenly feels concerned.

'I'll get cooking, then,' she smiles.

Arriving at their new house, Ajay and Abhay sprint up the stairs to the first floor where the family will live. They race around, poking heads in different rooms, and slipping on the shiny cool tiles. The house is so modern and big! There is glass on the windows, and enough rooms for the boys to each have their own.

'I bags this one!' Ajay yells happily. 'It's close to the kitchen so I'll be able to smell all the good smells.'

The hospital area is on the ground floor, still under construction. Builders have been working on it for the last few months, creating four separate rooms for patients as well as a brand-new operating theatre for Daddy and the other surgeons to work in. Once the construction work is finished, the hospital will sleep up to 12 patients.

'I can't believe it!' Daddy exclaims, gazing around. 'My own hospital, where I can choose to help anyone I wish to. I'm so happy,' he says, eyes filling.

He turns to Mummy.

'This couldn't have happened without you, Lata,' he says. 'Thank you.'

'Family hug!' Abhay calls, and the four of them huddle in each other's arms for a long warm moment.

*

The hospital is Ajay's parents' life. Murli starts operating at 6.30 every morning and works through until all the surgeries for the day are finished. If emergencies come in, he treats these patients too. He never says 'no' to anyone.

Ajay and Abhay see people arrive with horrible wounds, in pain, suffering. The injured and sick come in oxcarts with their family – sometimes as many as 15 people. They park in front of the hospital where they wait patiently for medical care.

To the boys' amazement, the families sometimes get out **Bunsen burners** and cook while they wait to see their father.

> A **Bunsen burner** is a type of gas burner usually used in science laboratories.

Mummy is fanatical about keeping the hospital clean. She says the hospital is only as good as its hygiene – otherwise people can leave sicker than when they arrive. She runs baths for patients and when Ajay asks about this, she says, 'Many of the people are quite dirty when they arrive. It's not their fault, it's because they don't have clean water or places to wash like showers or baths in their villages. They don't even have taps or basins most of the time.'

Ajay is 12 when he begins to spend time with his dad in the hospital.

'Is there anything I can do to help?' he asks one day.

Murli looks at him and thinks a moment.

'Well, yes, actually, there is. Would you like to be in charge of getting the surgical clothes ready for the steriliser?'

Ajay's chest fills. The blue surgical clothes are worn by all the doctors and theatre staff. This is important business!

*

Scrubs
Another name for the blue or green surgical clothes worn by hospital staff.

Over the next year, Ajay shadows his dad around the hospital. Every day after school, once he has eaten, he heads downstairs to do his job of preparing the **scrubs**. The more he sees and hears, the more fascinated he is by what his dad does. He listens as his father explains to patients the necessary procedure and what is involved. He sees people wipe tears of fear from their cheeks. He feels so much kindness in the way his dad speaks with his patients. And there are so many of them. Dozens, every day, day after day.

But despite the constant workload and pressure, Ajay never once sees his dad lose his cool. Not with patients or staff. And not with his family, either.

Ajay often witnesses patients paying his father for their treatment. They hand him a wad of money, or some notes and coins. Murli never counts it.

He just puts it in his pocket and thanks them.

One night Ajay asks how he knows if they're paying the right amount.

'If a patient short-changes me, Ajay, so be it. What is most interesting, though, is that the poor never, ever short-change me.'

Ajay stares at him, letting that sink in. 'Which means ... the wealthy sometimes do?' he asks.

Daddy doesn't respond, but Ajay knows the answer.

One morning, after he's finished his breakfast of roti and tea, Daddy turns to Ajay.

'You've been really helpful to me at work this year, Ajay.'

'It's so interesting, Daddy. I love being part of it.'

He smiles. 'Yes, I can tell. I've been thinking ... One of these days, I'm going to get a call in the middle of the night when there won't be another doctor available to help me. So, I'd like to teach you how to scrub, how to put on gloves and wear a surgical gown so you can be my assistant.'

'Your assistant *in the operating theatre?*' Ajay says. 'As in, being in theatre with you while you operate?'

Daddy nods. 'If you'd like that.'

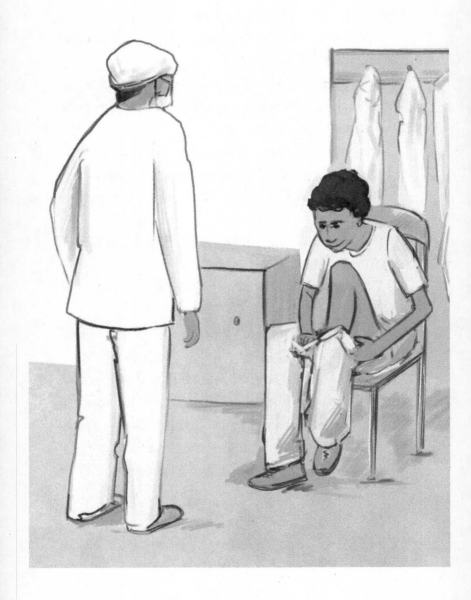

Ajay's eyes are wide with the thought of it – being in theatre with his dad during actual operations; helping people get better. He beams with pride.

'So I take it that's a yes, then?'

Ajay emits a squeak in the affirmative.

'Well, let's get to work then!

Daddy gives him a light blue smock and some loose pants.

'These are your surgical scrubs. Pop these on over your t-shirt and shorts,' he says. 'And then put on this theatre hat,' he continues, passing him a blue papery cap that looks like something old women wear in the shower.

'Right, good.' Daddy appraises his young theatre assistant. 'That's stage one.'

They head into the scrub area next to the operating theatre.

'This is stage two,' Daddy says. 'The surgical handwash.'

Ajay wonders how hard it can be to wash your hands that he needs to be taught? He's been washing his hands since … forever! Every time he goes to the toilet. Mummy is nuts about them washing their hands!

'Run the water until it is a comfortable temperature,' Daddy instructs. 'Now, wet your hands and arms, right up to your elbows.'

'Elbows? I thought we were washing our hands.'

'Yes, elbows. Bugs can live anywhere and we don't want any coming into contact with the patient while they're on the table. It's our duty to protect them from infection.'

Daddy points to the bar of soap.

'Now work up a really thick lather, Ajay, thick and foamy, and wash your hands and arms up to the elbows.'

Ajay does this and looks over at his dad at the next sink. He is still going.

'The longer, the better,' Daddy says, smiling. 'Keep washing for another couple of minutes.'

My skin is going to be raw after this, Ajay thinks, rubbing and scrubbing. He sneaks a look at Daddy again.

'Good. So now it's time to rinse. It's very important to keep your hands pointing up when you're rinsing, to make sure the water runs from your hands down to your elbows and not the other way around.'

Ajay can't believe this. Why is it so complicated?

'Why can't I just rinse off the soap like I do at home, in any direction?'

'Because the skin *above* your elbows is dirty – you haven't washed it, remember – you don't want that dirt to contaminate the clean area. So, it's very important, Ajay: keep your hands raised at all times. You'll see a lot of surgeons and theatre staff walking around like this, and that's why.'

His dad then points to a nailbrush and a nail pick. They each have one in front of them; Ajay had seen him open the individual packets earlier.

'Now clean under and around your nails, and when we're finished, we throw these away.'

'We *throw them away*?! But why? People could use these again; they're perfectly good!'

Daddy nods.

'I know. It seems wasteful, but it's the only way we can make sure we are completely clean before we operate on a patient, and the next patient after that. We must use a new nailbrush for every patient. They deserve to be protected from our bugs – they are so vulnerable when they're in theatre. We make an incision, and if the tiniest bit of bacteria were to get in there, they could get an infection, which would compromise their recovery. Do you understand?'

Ajay nods, looking unhappily at the pedal bin full of plastic packaging and once-only-used nailbrushes.

'Now for stage three.'

'Stage *three*?' Ajay said, 'Are you joking? There's more?'

'Oh, yes,' Daddy replies. 'Plenty more. Let's wet our hands and arms again...'

Ajay now knows that 'scrubbing' means washing his hands in the following ways repeatedly:
1. palms together;
2. with one palm over the back of the other hand, fingers interlaced;
3. with fingers in a 'monkey grip' position, clasping one another;
4. with rotational rubbing of each thumb; and
5. rubbing the fingertips of one hand into the palm of the other.

And once that is done, he has to use a rotating action up each arm to just below the elbow. And then rinse, keeping his hands raised above his elbows.

By the time they finish, Ajay knows he has never, ever properly washed his hands before.

'Now, you're scrubbed!' Daddy says.

Ajay nods slowly. The whole process has taken about half an hour.

'Do you have to do that before every single operation?'

'Every single time,' Daddy confirms.

Ajay feels his skin prickling and tingling.

'How do you have any skin left?!'

Daddy grins broadly.

'It keeps us tender.'

As Ajay leaves to go upstairs for dinner, Daddy says, 'Tomorrow, I'll teach you how to gown up. As you can imagine, it's not as simple as you think!'

All this before he could even go into theatre with Daddy! Why are there so many things he has to be patient for?

*

Ajay does have to help his father in the middle of the night – more than once.

The first time, he is under a warm, heavy blanket of sleep when Daddy wakes him.

'We have a sick young woman we must help, Ajay. She's in a lot of pain and needs to be operated on immediately.'

Ajay blinks a few times, then sits up. He staggers to his clothes drawer and pulls on shorts and a t-shirt. They head into the washing area adjacent to the theatre and he scrubs up as Daddy taught him, then puts on his surgical gown and gloves. They don't talk. He can tell from Daddy's face that he's thinking, planning the operation.

Once his father has **anaesthetised** the patient and is satisfied she is asleep and unaware, Ajay watches him paint the surgical area with rust-coloured disinfectant. He slowly makes an **incision** across the centre of her abdomen. This isn't the first time Ajay has seen an open body, but it is his first time to help with a flat blade called a **retractor**. Ajay focuses his mind to a pinpoint. He must help Daddy do his job as best as he possibly can.

The young woman's belly is swollen, almost as if she is pregnant, but Daddy says he has already examined her and she is not.

'Use the retractor to hold open the wound, please, Ajay,' he says.

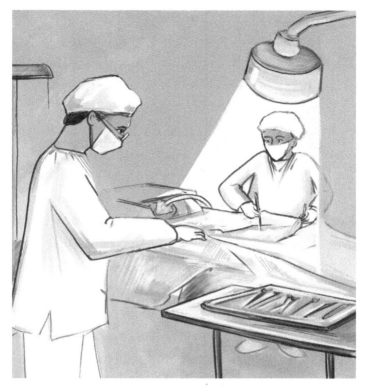

Ajay carefully applies the big silver surgical tool so his father can get access to the area.

Murli peers in. Using his instruments, he gently pulls tissue this way and that. And then he stops.

'There's the culprit,' he says, pointing with his gloved index finger. 'What organ is this, Ajay?'

Ajay looks. The organ is a long brown cone-ish shape and is to the right of the stomach.

'That would be … the liver?'

'Correct!' Daddy beams. 'And it is one very sick liver indeed at the moment. No wonder the poor woman has been in so much pain,' he murmurs.

'What's wrong with it?' asks Ajay.

'It's full of **hydatid cysts**. Each cyst contains the larval stages of a nasty tapeworm that dogs carry and is spread by their faeces.'

'Well, how did she get it then?' Ajay is confused.

'The infected dog's faeces gets into waterways where people wash clothes, so they come into contact with it and get sick. Hydatid disease can be fatal if the cysts leak or burst. We have to cut out the cysts, then give her some medicine to take.'

His dad gets to work. Ajay passes him instruments and uses a suction tool called an aspirator to remove the patient's blood pooling in the abdominal cavity when asked. Daddy cuts out several big cysts, and Ajay notes one is nearly the size of a tennis ball!

'You don't often see this disease in England and other developed countries, Ajay.'

'Why not?'

'Dogs aren't allowed to roam the streets, for one. Second, dog owners usually have the money to treat their animals for tapeworm with medicine that kills the worms, so it's just not that common.'

Ajay removes the clamps from around the woman's wound and watches as his dad neatly sews up the cut.

Daddy looks at him.

'See? I couldn't have done that without you. This patient would have suffered terribly until morning if I hadn't been able to operate on her. So, thank you, Ajay. You've really made a difference tonight.'

Ajay feels good.

'So now tumble back into bed. Don't worry about school in the morning. You can miss a day. Mummy or I will call them.'

*

Over the next few years, Daddy's confidence in him grows, and they work so well together that at some point – Ajay can't remember when, exactly – Murli stops being his dad and starts being his best friend.

Ajay absolutely loves being in the operating theatre. He never feels squeamish. And there's never a moment of doubt as to what he'll do when he finishes school.

6

Scaring the crows away

On school mornings, Ajay and Abhay rise early – they have lots to do! Ajay gets to work making sweet tea for the two of them while his brother lights a fire with sticks and cowpats to heat their bathwater.

Now in upper high school, Ajay loves everything in science. He soaks up knowledge like a sponge that shall never be squeezed out.

After school he races through lunch so he can join Daddy as soon as possible and sits in on as many surgeries as he is allowed, watching and listening carefully.

Apart from his father's work helping the sick get better, there are many people employed by the hospital – nurses, cleaners and administrative staff – all working together as a team.

Ajay sees that his parents have brought so much to this community, and why Daddy wanted to move back from England in the first place, even though it seemed crazy at the time. Mainly because of the pig toilet!

England. He thinks of it – less often than he used to, but still occasionally. He recalls London, with its round black cabs and red phone boxes – one of which Doctor Who commandeered for his Tardis. He remembers the grey skies and the beautiful old buildings lining the streets, and the tall, cone-shaped spires of churches. And the trips they did into the country, along winding narrow lanes dotted with hobbit cottages, and everywhere, everywhere, soft green hills. Ajay knows he will go back some day. But India is home now, and he's happy here.

*

'Daddy, I'm just going to take these dirty scrubs to the laundry,' Ajay says, his arms wrapped around a huge pile of green and blue surgical clothes.

'Excellent, thank you. Make sure you wash your hands afterwards.'

Ajay sorts the clothes into baskets as he's been shown to do, and chats with Rabhya who is folding clean washing.

'Where's Geetika?' he asks. 'She's normally here to help you.'

Rabhya tilts her head lightly. 'No, no, she's not in this week; she's been touched by the crow.'

Ajay's confused; he doesn't remember seeing any crows around.

That night when he's helping clean up after dinner, he asks his mum, 'Why wasn't Geetika at work today? I was in the laundry and she's always really nice to talk to.'

'Errr…' Mummy struggles to answer, then says, 'You can't speak to her at the moment, Ajay. She's been touched by the crow.'

Ajay is *so* confused.

'*What* crow?'

She stops and turns to him.

'Oh ... sorry, my darling. I mean, she's...' She stops again. 'It's women's business.'

He blushes. He knows a little about women's business – as much as any boy his age wants to know! But he doesn't know how it could keep Geetika away from work? Or from him talking to her? *Probably better not to ask*, he thinks. *Could be an embarrassing conversation.*

A couple of days later, when Geetika is still not back, he asks Murli about it.

'What does "touched by the crow" mean, Daddy?'

'Ah.' He puts his pen down. 'It's a figure of speech. It's another way of saying a woman is menstruating.'

Ajay feels awkward but his curiosity drives him on.

'So? Rabhya said that's why Geetika's not at work this week. But she can still work, can't she?'

'Well, yes, strictly speaking, yes, she can. Menstruation doesn't affect a woman's ability to do anything.'

'So why isn't she at work? And why did Mummy say I couldn't speak to her?'

Murli takes a deep breath. 'It's all to do with beliefs in India, Ajay. When a woman is menstruating she isn't allowed in the house – or in the hospital, in our case. At home, she has to sleep outside or on the floor. She's not allowed to cook or eat with the rest of the family and has to keep her plates and cup separate. And, if a relative dies, a menstruating woman isn't allowed to pay her respects. She can't go to the funeral or visit the grieving family.'

Ajay shakes his head. 'That's awful! Why? It doesn't make sense!'

'I know,' Daddy says. 'It's very sad. It has no foundation in science, but for some reason in Indian culture menstruation is seen as … a dirty or shameful thing. Some other cultures believe this too. Of course, it *isn't* dirty or shameful, not at all, Ajay, but that's what people here think, and it's what they've believed for centuries.'

Ajay keeps shaking his head.

Daddy goes on: 'Indian women won't even *talk* about menstruating. They refer to it as being "touched by the crow" even when they're talking to other women! The worst part of it, Ajay, is how much schooling and work they miss over the course of their lives because of this ridiculous belief. Every month a girl misses about five days of school and a woman the same number of days of work. That keeps women poorly educated, and poor.'

'So why do they tell anyone – that they're menstr – "touched by the crow", or whatever? They could just keep it a secret, couldn't they? I mean, no one would know, right?'

Daddy nods. 'You're right: it's nobody's business but theirs. But they're expected to self-segregate. Separate themselves from everybody else. Terrible.'

'Mummy doesn't.'

'No, that's because we know there's nothing wrong or shameful about a woman's body doing what it does naturally.'

Ajay goes outside to watch the world go by for a little while before dinner. **Rickshaws** trundle along the dusty road, dodging cows, cars and people. Blue-black crows bounce unsteadily on a nearby powerline. They *awwwww* at him.

A **rickshaw** is a three-wheeled bicycle with a covered seat for passengers behind the driver, used in many parts of Asia as a cheap alternative to taxis.

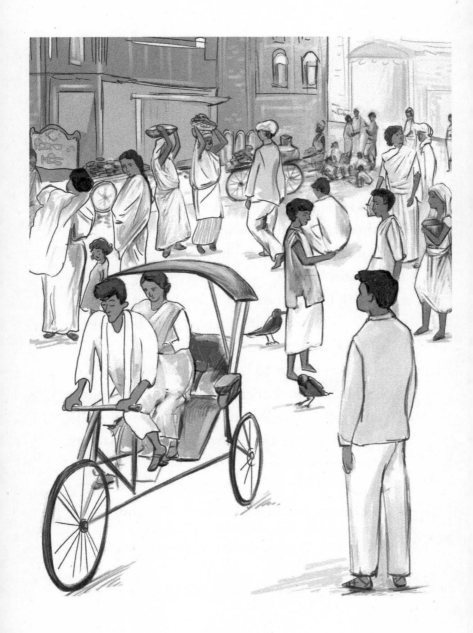

'Yaaaaaahhhhhh!!!!!' he yells at them. He picks up a rock and aims it right at the biggest crow. Misses.

*

Ajay has never questioned that he will go to university, nor what he will study there. There hasn't been a moment since he began working with his father in the hospital that he has not known he will become a doctor. Being so certain of where he is heading, Ajay doesn't need his parents to tell him to study hard. Just as his father did, he devotes long nights at his desk, his textbooks brightened by the light of a lamp. His hard work is rewarded when he gains entry to one of the country's best medical schools.

Mummy cries when he shows her the letter from the university in Pune. Daddy's eyes glisten with pride. The university is a two-hour drive from home.

That evening, Murli finishes work at six o'clock and puts a sign up on the hospital door saying it will re-open first thing the next morning. There has only been one other time he has done this – when Abhay got into university. Murli takes a taxi to Bhalod and gathers up his parents, Soma and Banabai, who are about to prepare their evening meal.

'Aai, Baba,' he hugs them. His gratitude is supersonic. 'Ajay has just been offered a place at the University of Pune.'

Banabai's face fills with wonder. 'Murli!' she says. 'Oh Murli!' She hugs him. 'You and Lata have given him good genes and have shown him what can be done with hard work.'

'Aai!' Murli protests. 'This began with your pot of copper coins. Please don't ever forget that. You and Baba are ... are ... *heroes*.'

Soma is sitting down, smiling.

'You educated one child,' Murli goes on, 'and now look at the ripples spreading from that one incredible decision.'

'The village worked together.'

'Lata is cooking a feast for us,' says Murli. 'I have a taxi just outside.'

Banabai says, 'I'll quickly change'.

Murli and Soma look at each other. Banabai *never* gets ready quickly.

'I said I'll be quick!'

Murli sighs with false impatience. 'Baba,' he winks. 'Please don't say you need to change too.'

Soma chuckles and waves the idea away.

'What you have done, Murli – the choices you've made, to study medicine, to go to England, to return to India – you have done us proud, my son. And your whole village.'

Banabai returns wearing a stunning gold-flecked sari. She reaches deep into a cupboard and brings out two huge jars of pickle. Her smile goes from ear to ear. 'That boy may eat all this pickle tonight as far as I'm concerned.'

'Let us celebrate,' Murli says, as they step out of the simple home and into the waiting taxi.

*

Ajay moves into the university's student accommodation and settles into a routine of going home to see his parents most weekends. Sometimes he takes one of his young student friends, reassuring them of how welcome they will be. There is always room around his family's table for an extra mouth, especially hungry medical students! The funny thing is, all these people call Murli 'Daddy', just like Ajay does. 'Yes, Daddy,' they say, when he shares his knowledge about a particular surgery. This habit continues even when they are much older and highly experienced doctors with families of their own; Murli is 'Daddy' to every one of Ajay's friends.

Ajay also always pays a visit to Aaji and Aajoba. He helps his dad out in the hospital and is increasingly able to take on more responsibility. One day, as they scrub for surgery, he says, 'Daddy, I'm thinking of specialising in **obstetrics** and **gynaecology** next year.'

Murli nods and looks across at him as he lathers his upper arms. 'Mothers and babies, very nice! Tell me more.'

'It's the inequality girls and women suffer,' Ajay says. 'It's wrong; I don't understand it. It begins the minute they're born and follows them all the way to their grave.'

'Yes,' says Murli. 'It should be unacceptable, but sadly it is widely accepted.'

'Well, I can't accept it.'

'Good. I'm glad to hear it.'

'Last week, Daddy...'

'Mmmm?'

'I was assisting a senior doctor at Pune Hospital. A woman was brought in suffering from a **haemorrhage** after her baby was born. The doctor indicated that I should explain the situation to the men who'd brought her in.'

Murli waits.

'I don't know if it was her husband or brother or friends or colleagues. Anyway, it was a pretty simple case. The patient needed some blood as she'd lost so much. I said to the men, "You can donate blood for her and she'll be okay".

'One of the men said to me, "But we're labourers. We can't donate blood, we'll get weak". I reassured them that giving blood doesn't make you weak. I explained that their blood would regenerate very quickly.'

'But they said, "No, we can't donate our blood for her". I said, "But why? She's dying. Without a blood **transfusion**, she'll die."

'And Daddy, do you know what they did? They just shrugged their shoulders. As if to say, *So be it.*'

Murli sucks in a big, slow breath. 'Oh, god.'

'I felt sick. I couldn't believe it. They were absolutely willing to let her die.'

'So, what happened?'

'I...I asked them to leave.' Ajay's shoulders drop low as he recalls the conversation. He rubs his hands hard. 'And then I went and drew a pint of my own blood and asked Rudra to donate a pint of his.'

Murli stops washing. 'And the patient?'

'She got the transfusion and recovered over the next couple of days. She's probably back at work now. We sent her home in a rickshaw.'

'And so it begins, Ajay,' Murli says, washing feverishly. 'A life of giving.'

Escalators
and love

As the plane lands at Heathrow Airport, Ajay notes the dark, dragging sky and the wet tarmac. The pilot announces that it's nine degrees in London. It takes Ajay a moment to compute that figure. Nine degrees, maximum. It was 37 degrees in Pune when he left!

But I'm not here to enjoy the weather, he thinks.

Entering the airport terminal, Ajay is agog. The building is shiny, as if it is brand new. There are televisions everywhere with flight details,

86

and billboards and moving signs on every wall. There are shops selling everything from Rolex watches to French perfumes to pies with mushy peas (which Ajay vows never, ever to eat).

There are people everywhere, going in every direction. There are escalators. Everywhere. He feels as if he's on a Snakes and Ladders board; short escalators, long escalators, and super-long (and terrifyingly high) escalators glide up and down. He watches people get on them a few times before attempting to do it himself. Then he inches forward, raises his foot and steps back. He can't do it – it's dangerous! These things gather people up, shunt them along on their tractor-style disappearing steps and then spit people off. Someone will die! Or lose a foot, at the very least.

Ajay takes the stairs that don't move. And finally makes his way out to the real world. He pulls his jacket tightly around him and tries not to think of his family, and warm India with its delicious food.

*

Ajay has returned to England, the place of his birth, to do more study. He is already a qualified doctor, specialising in obstetrics and gynaecology, but his work in India made him realise he needs to learn a lot more. He wants to get qualifications in **urological surgery** to help the desperate women he'd met every single day in his work in hospitals back home – women who'd had difficult births and needed surgery so they could live normally again.

What particularly frustrates him is that most injuries caused during childbirth are avoidable, yet they are common in India and other developing countries. The injuries are also treatable, yet they are regularly left completely untreated. One problem is particularly common: **obstetric fistula**.

This is a serious injury that can occur during childbirth. It leaves women **incontinent**, and as a result they are often shunned by their communities and even their own families. Some women are sent away from their own homes in shame and kept from their children. Many live with the condition for years – even decades – because they cannot afford to obtain treatment.

It's no life, Ajay thinks every single time he encounters such a woman. Surely there is something he can do to help?

Over the next few months Ajay works like a trojan. When he's not studying for his urology exams Ajay puts in a huge number of hours at the hospital.

While mastering the human body and its repair doesn't seem difficult for Ajay, he does seem to struggle with more everyday puzzles, such as England's fast-moving escalators, and those weird glass cabinets offering food and drinks called vending machines. They are both scary beasts and he has nearly injured himself in his half-hearted attempts to use them so far. Stepping off an escalator nearly ended with a spectacular fall, and trying to entice a drink from a vending machine in the hospital corridor almost caused the amputation of his hand. Ajay knows he will need both hands to make a good surgeon, that's for sure!

*

Ajay is relaxing with the weekend papers after passing his urology exams when he spots an advertisement for the position of Senior Registrar at an excellent hospital in Belfast in Northern Ireland. He reads through the job description. Yes, he definitely has all the qualifications – more, in fact, thanks to all his work in India, and now England, so he applies for the job.

A few weeks later he receives a phone call, the sing-song Irish accent of the caller completely throwing him. He can barely understand a word of what she is saying.

'Please, could you say that again?' he asks.

'Aye. Could yuu come inte hospital fer en interview? Fer the job?'

There's a long pause.

'Fer Senior Registror. Yuu did apply, didn't yuu?'

More pause.

'At Nerden Irelant General?'

It finally clicks. An interview for the job!

'Yes, *yes*! Sorry, my apologies. I'm still getting used to the accents here...'

'Aye, tat's orkey. So, is niyn o'clock Wednesday orkey for yuu?'

'Yes! Yes.' *Calm down, Ajay. You sound like a happy puppy.* 'Who should I ask for when I arrive?'

It's not just one person, but a panel of 13 senior doctors who interview him that Wednesday. Actually, they interrogate him. He needs a majority vote to get the job – so seven or more votes. Ajay is incredibly nervous. His heart is thumping and he feels perspiration trickling down his back during the very formal, and very long interview.

90

A couple of the doctors stare at him at the beginning as if he's some kind of oddity at the circus.

Ajay knows why they stare: he has dark brown skin. This isn't London, with its large communities of Indian Britons and curry houses on every corner. This is super-conservative Belfast. Here, in Northern Ireland, he *is* an oddity.

You have the skills, he reminds himself. And there can be nowhere harder to get above one's 'station in life' than India, surely? His father's story is the ultimate reminder of that.

Seven doctors vote for Ajay.

Six do not. It's very close, but he gets the job.

Those six dissenting voices are, for Ajay, almost louder than the seven who vote for him. He will show them what he can do; what can be achieved with hard work, and dedication, and passion.

*

He meets Paula on his very first day in the job and is a bit shocked when he realises she's a medical student, not a nurse. It's hard not to be impressed by a young woman who has made it into this very male-dominated medical world.

'High are yuu?' she says.

Ajay pretends he understands by nodding and smiling.

'Settling in orkey are yuu?'

'Getting there,' he says, hoping he heard her correctly. 'Looking forward to seeing some patients and meeting the other doctors I'll be working with.'

'I've been led to believe we've a lot to learn from yuu, Dr Rane. Great tings, apparently.'

Ajay can't hide the look of surprise from his face. He hopes he can meet her expectations! Paula has an impish red bob and cheeky hazel eyes. He smiles.

'Well, I hope I can share some of the things I've learned along the way with you all. And I know I'll learn a lot from the team here.'

'Well, welcome on board,' she says as the other junior doctors arrive and lots of introductions begin.

Then, just as the students and doctors are looking at the patient list for the day, there is a massive BOOM! in the distance. The hospital's windows explode in and debris flies across the room. Ajay's arms jerk up to protect his face and he looks around trying to understand what has happened.

Most of the staff are on the floor, some under the table, others covering their heads with their hands. A couple are whimpering. Paula has ducked down beside a cupboard.

'Is everyone alright?' Ajay asks quietly. 'Is anyone hurt?'

Slowly they get up, some carefully plucking away shards of glass. There is a shocked silence.

'What *was* that?' asks Ajay.

'A bomb,' Paula says matter-of-factly, tutting.

'A *bomb*?'

'**The Troubles**,' she explains. 'The **IRA**, probably.'

The Northern Ireland conflict was known as **The Troubles**, and lasted for around 30 years from the mid-1960s. The **IRA**, or Irish Republican Army, was a paramilitary organisation.

'Fer God's sake,' one of the students hisses, rearranging his clothes. 'No wonder the hospital's so busy! We'll have a flotilla of ambulances arrive in te next turty minutes, yuu'll see. It's nuthin' short of a civil war.'

'Yuu alright, Doctor?' Paula asks Ajay as the clean-up begins. 'Tat's a bit of a rude start, isn't it?'

She is kind. And smart. Just like his mother, Ajay thinks, and his grandmother. He nods at her and takes a breath.

Really? Is that feeling really what he thinks it might be? On the first day of his new job? For a student? In the aftermath of a bomb detonation?

It is, as Ajay likes to say, the beginning of an explosive relationship.

*

Initially, Ajay tries to ignore the distinct impression he gets from some of his patients that they are checking him out much like they might an alien from another galaxy. Their misgivings only fuel Ajay's ambition. He wants to dissolve any doubt anyone has in his abilities and he only has to think of his father to be reminded of why it is so crucial that he does so. His frequent telephone calls home, particularly with Murli in his short breaks between patients, help him stay on track. If an 'Untouchable' child could become a surgeon and own a hospital in India, then Ajay can overcome any hurdle he faces.

An **Untouchable** is someone belonging to the lowest caste in Indian society: the Untouchable caste (also called Dalit). It is now known as the Scheduled caste.

He and Paula get to know each other better both on the ward and outside the hospital, by going on long walks through Ireland's beautiful, undulating green countryside. Ajay tries very hard on these hikes to get close to one of the many black-faced sheep that trot through fields, but they scamper away whenever he approaches.

'Yuu buck eejit!' Paula declares on one attempt.

'I have no idea what you just said, but I think it was an insult,' he grins.

Paula puckers her lips and puts on her best Queen's English. 'It means, good sir: "You utter idiot!"'

'I just want to be friends with them!' Ajay says forlornly.

'Tey won't have a bar ot yuu. Don't ignore the body language, Doctor!'

They see hares hurrying, foxes skulking and deer on alert as they walk and talk and share their dreams with each other.

When he eventually gets up the courage to hold her hand, Ajay quietly says, 'You know, we have nothing in common. Beyond our work, I mean.'

Paula laughs. 'Wonderful, isn't it? Yuu're a Hindu and I'm a Catholic from Northern Ireland. It's nuts.'

'How are your parents going to take it?'

She pauses. Then her voice goes down a notch. 'They'll fall in love wit yuu, just like I think I might be.'

*

It takes Ajay five years to be able to follow what Paula's dad says without having to lip-read him. Initially, he asks Paula to translate – a lot.

'What does "Bout ye?" mean?' he whispers when her brother greets him one evening.

'It's standard Northern Irish for "How are you?",' she says. 'Same as "What's the craic?" That means, "What's happening?". Yuu'll be right in the thick o tings if yuu start speakin' like tat.'

They're a warm and loving family and they love their soccer. Every Saturday night the family watches the game together. Everyone has their own special seat, which doesn't change for anything, and the dog lies next to the fire, rolling onto his back occasionally in the hope of a tummy scratch. There's no seat for Ajay, though, so he lies on the floor next to the dog – nice and close for the odd scratch. After a few visits, Kay, Paula's mum, brings Ajay a footstool so he can rest his elbow whilst watching the soccer.

'Oooh, yuu know yuu're bein' accepted when Mam brings yuu a *special footstool*,' Paula declares, walking with Ajay to his car. She smiles from ear to ear. 'Yuu must be okay, Doctor!'

It's not long afterwards that Ajay proposes to Paula.

When she nods, eyes brimming, he says, 'You must come to India and meet my parents.'

Tears jumble down her cheeks.

Ajay adds, 'And try my grandmother's pickle. It's very – no: *very, very* – good.'

'When are we going?' she grins, the world opening up before her like a magical atlas.

*

Ajay and Paula marry in the pretty Irish village of Eire, in County Kildare. The area is known as a green haven for outdoor activities, including horse riding, fishing and walking – when it's not raining cats and dogs, which it often is!

The day they marry is the first of a lifetime of love for the young couple. Ajay's parents, especially his mum, are so very happy for him.

8

The Nurse of Nashik

Those early years in Ireland are happy. Ajay works hard and Paula studies even harder. However, The Troubles in Ireland mean that Catholics like Paula face a great deal of discrimination, and when she qualifies as a GP, Paula knows she will never get a job easily in her home country. All the good jobs at the time go to **Protestants**.

Protestants belong to Christian churches that rebelled (or protested) against the dominant Catholic Church. Many wars between Catholics and Protestants were fought in Europe and the British Isles. The most recent was in Northern Ireland which is still ruled by Britain.

Ajay sees how angry and upset Paula is every time she's knocked back for a job. She has worked so hard against the prejudices facing her – first in medical school and then in the hospital – just because she is a woman and a Catholic. But, desperate to help those people she knows need her skills, she keeps on studying, hoping that one day, her extra qualifications will give her a head start.

Seeing her close to tears one night when he arrives home from a long shift at the hospital, after she has missed out on yet another job, Ajay suddenly has a brainwave.

'Let's put way the textbooks for a while and see the world!'

She looks up at him in disbelief.

'We've both worked so hard till now; we need a break. We can go anywhere we like. Who knows where we'll end up or what will happen at the end of our trip!'

*

They pack clothes and guidebooks into backpacks and head into the global wilderness, exploring across continents for a glorious 18 months. They visit exotic places and go on daring adventures – sometimes some really scary ones. One day when scuba diving in the Red Sea – that warm, salty stretch of water between Egypt and Saudi Arabia – Paula looks around to show Ajay a beautiful, brightly coloured angelfish but realises he's no longer nearby. Panicking, she spins around and around in the water, looking below and above her and in every direction, but she cannot see him anywhere. She takes urgent action, doing an emergency ascent to the surface.

What she hadn't realised was that Ajay had in fact remained on the water's surface. As she breaks through the surface, fear etched on her face, he grabs her.

'What happened?' he asks.

She splutters, pulling off her mask. 'What do you mean? Where were you?'

'I was watching you, my love!'

Of course, they laugh about this for years to come, but at the time it wasn't funny at all.

*

The couple can't wait to visit India. Ajay is excited to show Paula the country of his childhood, and to introduce her to his relatives. The thick hot air with its pungent spicy, smoky smells hits Paula the minute she steps out of the plane and descends the steps to the tarmac after landing at Mumbai airport. On the drive into the city, she is astonished by the scene: there are masses of people everywhere, sharing the roads with tooting, jostling vehicles of every description – trucks, bicycles, buses and rickshaws. Men push carts piled high with goods, while cows saunter unhurriedly through it all. Her senses are both overwhelmed and excited, but also confused and shocked by the obvious wealth and poverty that exists side by side.

Ajay's parents welcome Paula warmly but some of his other relatives just stare at her. They are curious about this pale-skinned foreigner in their midst.

On their first night, they are invited to a dinner. Of course, there is no cutlery provided. On top of that, Indians don't eat with their left hand since it is a 'hand of ablution'. But Paula's left hand keeps moving towards her food, trying to help her right hand with its tricky new task. Unless you've practised since childhood, it's very hard to pick up rice with your fingers! In the end, Paula's left hand just can't stay out of it so she sits on it to make sure she doesn't accidentally use it!

It's also on this round-the-world trip that Ajay and Paula come to Australia for the first time, touring Queensland's sunny Gold Coast. They love it and vow to be back.

Their holiday over, they return to Ireland, and within weeks Ajay is offered a job as a specialist doctor in England. This is another big promotion for Ajay and he and Paula leap into the next phase of their working lives – 10 years in England.

*

Ajay is one of the youngest specialists in England, and Paula has landed a great job too, as a doctor, without any concerns of religious discrimination or bombs!

One night as they lie in bed Ajay says, 'Can you imagine how much better I would have done if my parents had stayed here in England and not moved us to India?'

Paula listens.

'What was my father thinking? He wasted those opportunities for us – I could have gone to some of the best medical schools in the world if we'd stayed here.'

'You sound angry.'

'I *am* angry,' Ajay says, feeling terrible as he says it. 'I know they wanted to do the right thing by the people of Bhalod but what about doing the right thing by their own children?'

'But you gained a lot by having those experiences, wouldn't you say?'

'Well, yes,' says Ajay, 'but at what cost? It was really traumatising being taken from our comfy life here and just dropped into a very basic existence in the village. Abhay couldn't go to the toilet for the first week; have I told you that story?'

Paula nods. 'You have, Ajay, a few times. But look at you now. I mean, seriously, you have one of the best jobs someone of your age could imagine.'

'No, I'd be way ahead of this if we'd stayed here. It was such a selfish decision of my father. And it was very hard for my mum. She loved England.'

So, to make up for what he thinks he has lost, Ajay decides to do yet more study while in England. He squeezes as much medical training he can into the 24 hours available to him each day – most of which are spent working in the hospital – and in the remaining time he begins new university degrees.

*

Years pass and Ajay is working himself into the ground. He has more letters after his name than there are in the **Cambodian alphabet** but, thankfully, Paula can see it for what it is: Ajay has lost his way. He's unhappy and dissatisfied.

Khmer is the language spoken in **Cambodia** and has the largest alphabet of any language, with 74 letters!

Paula determines to get her husband back on task, doing what has always been meaningful to him – and that's caring for women, especially those without the means to get the help they need.

'Ajay,' she says one evening.

He looks up from his book.

'I'm not sure we're doing our best work here.'

'What do you mean?'

'I feel we're needed more elsewhere. Where women can't get to specialist doctors easily, or can't afford to. Rural areas. Developing countries.'

Ajay puts the book down.

'I know. Everyone here has easy access to medical services and if they can't afford to pay, the government covers it. It's an excellent system. Really equitable. Unlike many other countries.'

Paula says, 'You know ... when we travelled, we really liked Australia. And there are thousands of women living in remote areas there who have to fly to one of the cities to see a specialist. Which means, let's face it, they probably don't.'

Ajay looks at her.

'I wonder if there are any jobs going there ... You could do so much good.'

'And you could, too,' he says.

'Yes, but you know what I mean. You're the specialist. I can go anywhere.'

Ajay closes his eyes for a moment, imagining life in northern Australia where there are so many remote towns and communities. He sees red dirt and turquoise waters and can almost feel the searing heat on his skin.

'Are you serious? I mean, are you sure you want to do that? It would be a massive change from life here.'

Paula's eyes twinkle as only they can.

'Time for a challenge, Dr Rane.'

*

And that's it. In 1996, they land in Townsville, Queensland.

'Where are all the people?' Paula stares as they drive from the airport. Palm trees sway over tropical green foliage. It's sticky and Paula starts to flap a folded newspaper to cool her face.

'Hang on, I'll turn up the AC.' The taxi driver swivels a knob on the dash and cool air pumps towards the back seats. The population of Townsville has grown to around 85,000,' he says. 'It's boomin' – hard to find a park at the shopping centre sometimes!'

It doesn't take long for Ajay and Paula to find a pretty house to rent not far from the beach. On clear days in Townsville, which boasts over 300 days of sunshine a year, they can even see the gorgeous tourist destination, Magnetic Island, from the mainland.

'If it weren't so insanely hot, it would be perfect,' Paula says, waving a small fan she keeps with her across her face.

'It's so good after the bleak skies and freezing winters of Ireland and England!' Ajay exclaims, hugging her.

'I'll get used to it, I know,' she sighs.

Ajay is very warmly welcomed by the medical community in Townsville, and through Townsville Hospital he's able to offer his specialist services to not only the women of the small city but all those in the regional areas beyond. Some drive a 16-hour round-trip – eight hours each way – to have a 15-minute appointment with him. Ajay is amazed by their determination. And grateful too, because, with their trust, Ajay is able to start making the kind of difference he has always wanted to – life-changing and life-saving differences.

*

But Paula's medical career takes a completely different turn. Australia, it turns out, does not recognise her Irish qualifications. Six years of study at medical school and experience working as a GP doesn't cut it. So, to work as a doctor in Australia, Paula is told she'll have to re-train from scratch.

It's a terrible blow. She calls Ajay at work to tell him the news.

'How can this be right?' Ajay says. 'You're a qualified doctor, trained and with experience in the UK!'

Paula nods into the phone, trying unsuccessfully to swallow her tears.

'And this country is crying out for more doctors, especially in regional areas – like northern Queensland!'

She swipes her face. 'I'm not giving up. I'll take the Australian medical exams. It just means I can't work for a bit longer.'

To see Paula treated like this is heart-breaking. What makes it worse is the guilt Ajay feels about the wonderful position he has found here in Townsville – largely thanks to Paula's suggestion that they leave England.

Paula is true to her word and doesn't give up. She has taken very similar exams before and believes she will be able to pass these if she just puts the work in. And work she does.

Never one to fritter away time, Paula also gives birth to their two children during these years. Townsville is now home to the Rane family.

*

In the early 2000s, a doctor Ajay had trained with as a young man in India calls him.

After the usual catch-up conversation, the now-senior doctor asks Ajay if he would return to Maharashtra to train a group of doctors, himself included, in the special surgeries he does to help women who are injured during childbirth.

'I would love to do that,' says Ajay.

'There's a big group of us. We are very keen to learn from you and as you know there is so much need for these skills here.'

'Yes, yes, I understand. I would love to help in any way I can,' says Ajay.

'Thank you, Ajay, we are so appreciative. I'd like to arrange a local medical conference around your visit too, so I'll start getting things in place for that. We look forward to seeing you in Nashik!'

Several months later, Ajay flies out to Nashik (pronounced 'Nazik') to treat local women and teach interested doctors what he knows. This is the kind of challenge Ajay naturally embraces and he insists on doing the work **pro bono**. He's always happy to have

> **Pro bono**
> Working without charging a fee.

an excuse to go back to India, to be part of that colourful, dirty, smelly, vibrant place again, with the best food in the world.

The doctors greet him at the airport and offer to take him to the fancy hotel they've booked him into.

'No, no, I want to see my patients,' says Ajay. 'We're going to operate tomorrow, so I want to see them today.'

The doctors look at each other. 'Right now?'

'Yes,' Ajay nods. 'I want to see them now, please.'

One of the local doctors calls the clinic and arranges for the patients to be ready.

When Ajay arrives, he sees women sitting on the floor against a wall, in a long line. They are all waiting for him.

Ajay smiles warmly at them. They are all poor. They are filthy. He knows they have been treated terribly to this point, but their faces are full of hope.

He reaches into his bag and pulls out a bundle of clean white sheets. Ajay turns to the doctors. 'These are what I call dignity sheets. This is the first thing I want to teach you. Never examine a woman without a sheet covering her.

'Because of their medical problems, these women have been given no respect, treated as though they have no value. That stops here, the minute they come into your care.'

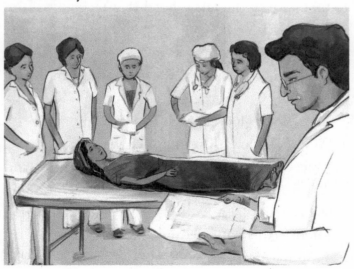

It is a long day but Ajay sees every one of those patients, the other doctors – most of whom are women – standing around him, observing, taking notes and asking questions. Finally, the last patient climbs up onto the examination bed. It's clear from the state of her that she is an extremely poor beggar. She smells awful. When Ajay examines her, he sees that she has a very large hole in her bowel that is leaking faeces.

Turning to the other doctors, he says, 'Look, I can fix this, but I can't teach this particular surgery, as it's very complicated. But I'm very happy to operate on this patient.'

The doctors speak among themselves. Then they say to Ajay, 'Let's do all the other surgeries first, as we want to learn from you. Then, if we have time, you can operate on this woman.'

Ajay says, 'I'm in your town, at your invitation. I'll do what you ask me to do.'

Then another voice comes into the conversation. It's the patient on the table. Incredibly, she speaks English – and well. Very clearly, she says, 'If you don't operate on me, I will kill myself'.

Everything in the room changes. No one moves or speaks. Ajay turns to the woman. He is appalled to realise how many things he and the other doctors have assumed about her.

She's a beggar in a small village of India ... who speaks English.

Ajay feels terrible shame. Tears spill from his eyes.

'I am so sorry. I didn't realise you understood English.'

'I'm a nurse,' she says. 'It's the fistula that's thrown me on the dung heap. They took my baby away from me, my husband threw me out of the house, and now I have to gather food on the garbage heaps to survive.'

It is one of the most powerful moments of Ajay's life. He vows to help her.

The next day they do surgery after surgery. It's a marathon of incisions and stitches and as the day heads into the late afternoon Ajay fears he will run out of time for his special patient.

'Where is the other patient, the nurse with the fistula?' he pleads with the local doctors at the end of the day.

'Sorry, Doctor, we have finished the patient list, we can't do any more now.'

Ajay has promised to give a lecture to local medical staff and students at 6.30 that evening. He goes to the lecture theatre feeling very unsettled. He keeps thinking about the nurse. He mingles with the guests before the lecture, wearing a smile as he moves from one group of people to the next. But he can't relax; things are not right.

He recognises an old friend from medical school in India, also a gynaecology specialist. He has not seen her in years! They begin chatting, catching up on all their news.

'I'm married to a surgeon,' Daksha says.

'Oh, that's great,' says Ajay, a thought coming into his head. 'So … do you have a hospital?'

'Yes, yes,' she says casually. 'We have trauma patients, obstetrics, childbirth.'

'So, you work 24/7?'

'Yes, yes.'

'And … do you have an anaesthetist?'

'Oh, yes, 24/7,' Daksha says happily.

'Lovely,' says Ajay, standing up a little straighter. 'I would love to operate in your hospital right now.'

She looks at him.

'What do you mean?'

'I have a patient.' He lowers his voice. 'She needs an urgent operation. I'll pay for it.'

Daksha looks directly at Ajay, and in that instant, understands that he is serious.

'Of course,' she says, face changing. 'Not a problem.'

Ajay gives the lecture. He is fired up and it shows. Despite his exhaustion from the last two days of work, he is energised. As soon as he finishes his speech, he excuses himself and heads towards his old friend.

They hightail it out of there.

The first thing to do is find the nurse-patient. They ask a few people who give them directions, but the labyrinthine slums are impossible to navigate. Finally, they invite a couple of locals into the car to help them, and they find the patient after a few minutes of weaving up and down lanes of makeshift homes, little more than the size of a family tent.

Her face upon seeing them is a vision. Never has Ajay felt such purpose.

As Daksha drives them to the hospital Ajay asks his patient a few questions. She has eaten something recently, so he will have to wait until midnight to do the operation. When they arrive at the hospital, they are met by an anaesthetist Daksha had arranged while Ajay was delivering his lecture.

It takes Ajay four-and-a-half hours to operate on the nurse – it's now 4.45 in the morning. The operation is successful and she will be able to live a normal life once her body has healed from the surgery.

Outside the theatre, he cleans up and sits down to a cup of extra sweet milky chai tea. Daksha comes into the staffroom as he is mid-mouthful and says, 'Ajay, your car is here to take you to the airport. Your flight leaves in two hours.'

They hug warmly, Ajay thanking her for making the operation possible.

'You are amazing,' she says. 'Please come back to Nashik soon!'

Ajay sits in his seat on the plane, watching the sun rise over the city. He feels as if he's just won the lotto. He feels alive. Supremely useful.

I want to feel like this more, he says to himself. *It doesn't get better.*

Adopting 53 children

Back in Australia treating women from far and
wide in Queensland, and raising his young family
with Paula, Ajay is strongly driven to do more and
more humanitarian work, especially in India. He

now makes regular trips to
the **Subcontinent** and it's on
one of these that he visits a
hospital in the slums of the
city of Chennai.

> India and Sri Lanka
> are often called the
> **Subcontinent.**

Despite spending most of
his childhood and early life in India, Ajay is always
shocked with each visit by the poverty so many

people live in. Ajay, on the other hand, is staying in a smart hotel with a big bed and several restaurants to choose from. He has spare pillows and an extra blanket in the wardrobe. There are bottles of clean water placed in his fridge every day. (He has to keep reminding himself: *never drink the water from the tap. Ever.*)

It's a country of paradoxes, he thinks as he walks to the hospital, seeing people pick over huge piles of rubbish right next to the tin-and-cardboard shelters they call home. Shoeless children play in filthy streams, while their mothers wash clothes in the same water. *There are the very poor and the very wealthy in India*, Ajay decides. *There is no in-between.*

The concrete exterior of the Kasturba Gandhi Hospital is streaked with mould. A woman stands at the front door.

'Hello, Dr Rane!' Dr Raji welcomes him. 'Thank you so much for coming.' She has bright, warm eyes. Ajay likes her immediately.

Inside, Ajay sees a big, dirty room with eight metal-framed single beds. They have sagging, heavily stained mattresses without sheets. A pregnant woman sits on the edge of one. There are no curtains separating the beds, though there are rails where curtains would hang from. There is no privacy. The metal trolley that would normally carry medical equipment is rusty and bare – there is literally nothing on it.

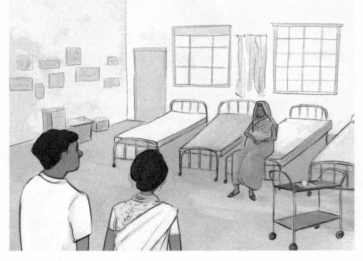

'My work here is with the local women,' Dr Raji explains. 'Some are pregnant, and some have just had babies and have untreated injuries from the birthing process. Fistulas. Nowhere else will treat them. Here, all our doctors are women. We look after them as best we can.'

Ajay nods. He feels so very sad.

'I read a little about the hospital last night …
you're a gynaecologist, aren't you?' he says. 'And
the first female urologist in India, I believe. That's
really something.'

Raji says, 'Yes, Dr Rane, that's true, but there is
only so much I can do. I am one person, but the
population in this area is very, very big. Millions,
just in this area. The theatre in our hospital is
basic. We don't have much equipment, not even
the simplest things like gloves – we have to re-use
gloves.'

She smiles and takes a breath. 'For those women
we can't operate on, we focus on teaching them to
manage their symptoms.'

'Symptoms they shouldn't have to manage – they
shouldn't have these problems at all,' Ajay says,
knowing she knows this.

'I know. It's so frustrating.'

Ajay looks around. He knows that this place
needs more money, more equipment. But it needs
more than that. Giving the hospital a generous
donation would make him feel better in the short
term, but wouldn't help the bigger problem, which
is the way local women and their families and

the medical profession in general thinks about women's health.

'We have to educate the local doctors and nurses, Raji. We have to improve the care these women receive during childbirth, and bring midwives into the picture,' he says.

'Yes,' she says, 'I couldn't agree more, but the male doctors don't listen to me when I suggest these things.' She shakes her head.

'And that's all part of the problem,' Ajay says. 'The total inequality.'

He looks around.

'And you've been here for how long, Raji?'

'Since not long after I qualified.'

'So your whole working life, dedicated to these women?'

Raji nods.

He takes a breath.

'Would you be willing to let me work with you, to try to change some of the really ingrained thinking out there? It will take some money, and lots of education and lots of time. We will need to be patient.'

Raji is nearly speechless. Ajay's words are music to her ears.

She eventually speaks, voice breaking with emotion. 'Of course I'd be willing – I would love your help!'

'First things first,' Ajay says, feeling better already. 'You invited me today to meet a few of your patients, so let me see them and then we can plan our hearts out.'

Raji indicates down a corridor, and Ajay looks.

Sixty women are lined up, waiting to see him. Ajay expected to be here for one hour. He looks at the sea of hopeful faces and knows two things: he will be here much longer than one hour, and he will bring Paula here next time he comes. Paula has finally completed her medical degree in Australia and is working as a GP in Townsville. Ajay knows she will love Raji and the incredible work she is doing.

*

Ajay's next visit to Chennai comes around sooner rather than later because he makes sure of it, and, just as he thought, Paula and Raji hit it off right from the word go, as if they have known each other forever.

And so, with Raji's blessing, Ajay and Paula pretty well adopt the place. They begin to visit

three or four times a year on a mission to renovate
it, bringing around 350 kilograms of hospital sup-
plies and equipment each time – sheets and
blankets, surgical equipment, educational bro-
chures, as well as posters to stick up on the walls.
Sometimes it becomes a family affair and their
children, and Murli and Lata – and even Paula's
parents from Ireland – join them for massive
working bees. They noisily, joyfully paint walls,
clean out cupboards, replace old beds and install
medical equipment.

'It's miraculous!' Raji says, walking into every
room and looking around with a smile she cannot
wipe off her face. 'It's the most wonderful make-
over I could have ever hoped for.'

Each time they leave, Raji literally weeps, with gratitude for all that they have done and sadness that they will not be by her side for the coming months.

At each visit, they also spend time training and educating the mainly women doctors and hospital staff about childbirth injuries and how to prevent these, as well as how to treat them if they do occur. Ajay gets his medical colleagues from Australia to donate their time and expertise to the cause, and they run workshops for all involved.

It's a real turning point. With donated money, Raji and her colleagues build a fistula ward with dedicated staff ensuring the patients have dignity and privacy. Next come new operating theatres with air-conditioning and state-of-the-art lighting.

In 2007, the local government names this new ward the Paula Rane Fistula Ward. There is an official ceremony attended by the Minister for Health and other local dignitaries, as well as all the hospital staff. There are speeches thanking all involved and addressing the plight of poor women. Despite being asked to say a few words, Paula declines. She is a shy person and simply wants the lives of local women and babies to improve. It's a very special moment for everyone there.

Within five years their new model of care has worked so well that the number of local women presenting at the hospital with obstetric fistulas has massively reduced.

Raji and her team of doctors and nurses are now able to keep most local women healthy and well.

Ajay looks proudly at the plaque bearing Paula's name.

'One day someone will say: good people did good work here.'

He squeezes Paula's hand.

The hospital now looks after between 20,000 and 40,000 women a year. In 2016, Ajay is awarded the Mahatma Gandhi Pravasi Award for Humanitarian Work in Women's Health. He says Paula's encouragement and support is behind everything he does.

*

But of course, Paula and Ajay's work is never done. There's no hammock-swinging for these two, because guess what? There's an orphanage next door to the hospital in Chennai. And Paula can't continue to walk past it.

Inside are 53 girls, abandoned by their parents, some of whom are too poor to care for any more children.

Sadly, though, many more girls than boys are given up for adoption in India. In some cases this is because boys are presumed more likely to contribute to the family income – they are considered superior workers to girls. Girls are also more expensive to raise than boys, needing a generous **dowry** to offer when they get married.

Dowry
The money or goods that a woman brings to her husband or his family in marriage in some cultures – it used to be common in most cultures across the world.

'These children...' Paula says to Ajay.

He breaks out in a sweat.

'Can we do something to help them? Or ... I suppose we could take them home. To Townsville.'

'Paula,' Ajay says, pretending to be calm. 'There are 53 children here.'

'I know,' she replies. 'And each one of them is a human being. Have you had a look around?'

'No,' Ajay looks at his shoes. 'I'm not sure I can bear to.'

'Well, they have to bear living here, so let's go.'

'Now?'

Paula pokes her head around a door that says MANAGER.

Shanti has been working there for more than a decade.

'I feel like I am Mummy to some of them,' she says. 'They are all such lovely children.'

She explains that every night she leaves a wicker basket outside the orphanage door for women who feel they can't keep their babies. 'Otherwise, the baby is left somewhere she won't be found – in the bush, or a bin – and many die. It's not their fault – and they are often perfectly healthy children. But they are girls.'

Ajay has heard of this practice and feels sick seeing it so close up. After all, as an obstetrician, his job has been to help thousands of women safely give birth to healthy babies.

'We want babies to live, no matter their sex,' Shanti says, patting the baby she's holding. 'Here, we believe girls and boys have the same value.'

Paula looks at Ajay. Ajay looks at Paula.

'Can you show us around, Shanti?' he asks. 'If you have time?'

'Yes,' she says, and then a baby starts crying. 'Would one of you be able to pick up Neera?'

'I would love to,' Ajay says, and heads straight to the cot.

Another little roar emanates from a cot on the other side of the room.

'Oh, Keerthi, really? I just gave you a bottle!'

'I'll get her,' Paula says, and scoops up the little body.

Ajay and Neera, Paula and Keerthi, and Shanti and the baby head into the next room, where 20 or so school-aged girls are crowded around only two much-thumbed textbooks. The eldest girl is explaining to the others what she knows about fractions.

Ajay and Paula observe for a while and are impressed by the composure of the girls and the warmth of their carers.

After the tour, around cups of tea, Ajay asks, 'What do you most need here to improve life for the girls?'

Paula says, 'And we mean not just today or this year, but beyond that.'

*

Over the coming years, Ajay and Paula send dental kits and laptops, and buy a scooter for the orphanage so the kids can get to school. Unsurprisingly, ensuring the girls get an education is a priority for them.

The orphanage remains close to Paula and Ajay's hearts, and they continue to be closely involved with it to this day. When they visit, they feel as if they are visiting their extended family.

10

Poo, Bollywood and chillies

As you know by now, Ajay knows everything about women's health and babies and all that stuff. But there's something else he loves to talk about. Pooing.

So, let's get into it. Don't be shy. We all do it, hopefully once a day or so. So, no need to feel embarrassed!

In Australia, most people use a traditional western toilet, which most dads seem to think of as their personal 'throne' or kingdom. But you can take off the crown, loo-hoggers, because it turns out this toilet structure is not the best design for our bodies.

'The fact is,' Ajay explains, 'our internal human plumbing prefers the knees-up approach when pooing.'

Well, that's certainly saying it like it is!

'There's nothing better than a good old "knees up",' says Ajay. 'Just ask your bottom.'

Oh, o-kay...

'It helps the poop move through and out of the body more easily.'

In developing countries – like India, for example – pretty well everybody uses the squatting position. And we know Ajay has spent a lot of time in India. So, he decides to do what any sane full-time medical doctor and professor who also supports a hospital and an orphanage in another country would: he goes back to university to study – again – and this time does a PhD. On bowel movement.

(That's more letters after his name. About how to poo. But it's not about the letters. It's about teaching the likes of us how to poo properly. Because it's kinder to our body.)

During his research, Ajay designs an adjustable squat platform that can be used with a western-style toilet. The platform is called 'Duneze' (think of 'dunny') and sits on the floor below the loo. The person sitting on the loo puts their feet on Duneze, which raises their knees – copying the body position of a squat.

Ajay calls it a 'poovolution' and says it solves many of the problems throne-users often suffer from, including constipation and **haemorrhoids**. Yuck! Who needs those?

*

From his work with the poorest women in the world to his work on poo, you should know by now that Ajay loves to surprise us. And to keep on surprising us. So, he and a colleague do exactly what you'd expect of a couple of Australian stethoscope-wearing surgeons: they write, direct and produce a Bollywood film!

While Bollywood conjures up images of colourful dancing and Indian pop hits, Ajay's film has a serious side. *Riwayat: When Traditions Kill* explores the discrimination and neglect of women from birth to death.

It also examines the terrible but widespread cultural belief in India and other developing countries that female babies are 'worthless'. Even to the point that, in some cases, pregnancies are terminated when the ultrasound scan shows that the baby is female.

Ajay and his colleague, Associate Professor Sanjay Patole, hear a great deal of this practice in their work as doctors in India. It's not limited to the poorer people; it's also common among the wealthy. And it doesn't matter if people are literate or illiterate. It has nothing to do with religion or caste. The practice is simply cultural tradition. And it's a huge problem in India and China.

Sanjay was one of the first people Ajay met in Townsville and the two doctors had hit it off straightaway. Even though they now live on opposite sides of Australia, with Sanjay in Perth, they keep closely in touch. And when these two eminent doctors of mothers and babies read in the world's leading medical journal, *The Lancet*, an estimate of the number of female babies being terminated, they decide something must be done. As human beings, husbands and fathers, Ajay and

Sanjay want change. As doctors, they must try to begin this change.

'It's intolerable,' Sanjay says in a phone call to Ajay. 'How can the modern world permit this?'

'The practice is so ingrained, isn't it,' Ajay says, 'These are such common, deeply held beliefs – the value of a male child over a female. When I bring this up with Indian doctors on my visits, most deny that it happens much in their region.'

'But the figures say otherwise! *One hundred million* girls have not made it into the world because of this practice!'

'I know. My brain can't even imagine that many people. I think there's huge denial about this, Sanjay. It's going to be a hard nut to crack.'

'And to think that here, at the women's hospital, I will spend weeks trying to keep just one tiny, premature baby alive.' Sanjay pauses. 'A hard nut, you say, Ajay. Well, you know what, that's my kind of nut.'

*

The doctors know they need to reach the masses. So, there's only one place to go: Bollywood. A full-blown Bollywood extravaganza, with glorious

135

costumes and vibrant singing and dancing – now *that* has a chance of reaching a big audience.

Ajay writes a script for the movie, which traces the lives of three very different women.

The doctors make multiple trips to India; 14 in two years for Sanjay. They foot the production bill themselves. Sanjay has a brother in the film industry in Mumbai who helps them secure the country's top singers and actors.

It's fair to say that Ajay Rane is not very well known as an actor. In fact, he's never acted before in his life, apart from in school plays, and one of those roles was as a tree. Which didn't move or speak, because: tree. But he has always really *really* wanted to be in a movie, so he and Sanjay decide to make his next dream come true, and ta-dah! Ajay has a brief **cameo** role in *Riwayat*.

> **Cameo**
> A short performance or appearance in a play or film by a celebrity (or, in this case, a doctor).

Riwayat opens in India at more than 250 theatres. The film wins 14 international awards, including the prestigious Jury Prize at the Cannes Film

Festival, and is shown at acclaimed film festivals in Berlin, Monaco and Cairo.

Ajay says of the film, 'All we want is to save just one life. That's reward enough.'

*

When a surgeon is operating, they sometimes chat with their theatre staff. You can imagine the sort of thing:

[long incision]

How was your weekend?

Good, had a nice round of golf.

[general poking and prodding around using long stainless steel surgical instruments]

It's when he is operating in Hyderabad in India, however, that Ajay's theatre assistant says:

My brother grows the world's hottest chillies.

Keeping his hands perfectly still, Ajay asks, *Seriously? The world's hottest?*

She nods.

Scalpel, please.

She passes the cold instrument.

It's in the Guinness Book of World Records.

That's ... amazing. Forceps, please.

That evening after work, Ajay detours to the local library. He's a little dubious about his colleague's claim, so wants to fact-check it. He scours the bookshelves until he finds the latest volume of the *Guinness Book of World Records*. Flicking the pages to the section on chillies, he sees a photo of the hottest chilli in the world held by a man from Hyderabad – his theatre assistant's brother!

Somehow, Ajay turns this into his next challenge. After he returns to Townsville, he gets permission from the Department of Agriculture to begin cultivating chillies on his and Paula's farm in Bluewater, about 30 minutes' drive from home.

'The hottest chillies in the world grow in Bluewater now,' he says to Paula with a satisfied grin.

*

Of course, for someone like Ajay, the work is never done.

Ajay continues his core work and is part of a global push to end obstetric fistulas by 2030. Around two million women around the world currently live with the injury – mainly from poor families in developing countries.

Ajay Rane, the son of Murli, the 'Untouchable' who was the only child of his village to go to high school and university, becoming a surgeon who built and ran his own hospital. Ajay Rane, now a great Australian citizen, was awarded Order of Australia (OAM) in 2013; was a finalist for the Australian of the Year in 2012; and was made an Honorary Fellow of the American College of Obstetricians and Gynaecologists in 2020 – among other honours.

Ajay Rane: let the wonderful work and the accolades continue. And the poo pep-talks. And the chillies. And the joy.

Postscripts

Postscript one

Ajay's parents, Murli and Lata, lived in India for the rest of their lives.

Lata died suddenly while working in the hospital she and Murli set up.

Murli was devastated by Lata's death. He carried on working for as long as he could. Ajay then came and looked after his father right to the last breath.

'It was an honour to care for him,' he says. 'He was an inspiration. Their hospital is still called the Rane Hospital, even though there are no Ranes there!' Ajay says, laughing. 'What a legacy my parents left.'

Postscript two

In 2018, Ajay was preparing for a big international medical meeting in Rio de Janeiro, Brazil. Ten thousand medical professionals would attend.

The organising crew said to him, 'Wouldn't it be brilliant if we could get a fistula patient to come and speak to the audience, to share her experiences?'

Ajay thought about it. He recalled one special patient in particular. *Come on, that was nine years ago!* he told himself. He put his hand on the phone, lightly. It was a long shot.

He heard the phone at the other end connect, then the voice of Daksha, his doctor friend in Nashik who'd let him operate on that very last patient – the nurse who spoke English – that night in her hospital.

'Do you remember that lady we operated on in your hospital?' he asked. 'The nurse?'

'Yes!' she said. 'Of course! Do you want to talk to her?'

'What?!'

'I've employed her as my nurse – right here in the hospital.'

Incredibly, Ajay spoke to her, and she remembered him, of course, and he heard her weep with gratitude down the phone.

'Would you...?' Ajay explained the invitation. 'It will be a big group,' he said. 'I mean *big*.'

The woman generously – bravely – wonderfully! – agreed to Ajay's invitation, and the conference organisers paid her fare to fly to Rio. She walked onto the enormous stage and stood behind the podium. It's a place she never would have thought she would find herself. There were huge TV screens behind her and to either side so the doctors sitting all the way up at the back of the auditorium could see her.

The nurse spoke to the huge gathering of doctors – international specialists, as well as younger doctors – about her experiences as a fistula victim. She told of her constant pain and shame, of being rejected by everyone and of scrabbling around in the rubbish heaps trying to stay alive.

Then she described life after her surgery, as someone who was again considered to be worthy of human society. She had since found a partner and had a baby.

Tears slipped down Ajay's cheeks as he watched her address the group. The eyes of audience members around him glistened with wonder and hope. Ajay's mind flicked back through his life. Without his father, he would never have had this incredibly privileged career of healing and giving, which in turn was thanks to his grandmother's determination and a community of poor cotton farmers who sacrificed their own comforts so just one of them could get ahead.

And one became many.

Postscript three

Ajay and Paula's son, Ben, is finishing his medical degree and their daughter, Tara, is studying public health. And so the ripples of Soma and Banabai's vision continue to spread.

Glossary

- **Anaesthetic:** A medical drug given to a patient before a medical procedure, ensuring they cannot feel the pain of the operation.

- **Consultant:** A senior doctor who has completed all of their specialist training and has been placed on the specialist register in their chosen speciality.

- **Gynaecology:** The branch of medicine dealing with the anatomy, physiology, and diseases of women, especially those affecting the reproductive organs.

- **Haemorrhage:** The medical term for bleeding or blood loss.

- **Haemorrhoids:** Swellings within the rectum or around the anus that consist of enlarged and swollen blood vessels. Also called piles.

- **Hydatid cysts:** Hydatid cysts cause hydatid disease (also called hydatidosis or echinococcosis), a potentially serious and even fatal condition. The cysts contain the larval stages of a tapeworm that infects dogs and other canines. The tapeworm eggs are shed in the faeces of infected animals, and then people can become infected by swallowing the eggs. This can be a result of handling the infected dog or eating contaminated food or water. (Queensland Government Health website, 2021.)

- **Incision:** A surgical cut.

- **Incontinent:** When a person can no longer control their bladder and/or bowel.

- **IRA:** The Irish Republican Army was a paramilitary organisation that sought to end British rule in Northern Ireland. The United Kingdom declared the IRA a terrorist organisation.

- **Obstetric fistula:** This condition is often caused by lengthy or obstructed childbirth. You can get a bladder fistula or a bowel fistula or both. This is where urine or faeces or both leak through the genital tract.

- **Obstetrics:** The area of medicine concerned with caring for and treating women in, before, and after childbirth

- **The Troubles:** The term refers to the political violence and conflict in Northern Ireland between the Catholic Nationalists who wanted a united Ireland, and the Protestant Loyalists who wanted to remain a part of Britain (UK). Catholics were in the minority in Northern Ireland and did not have equal opportunities in politics, jobs or education.

- **Transfusion:** When blood is taken from one person and given to another, because their own supply is depleted.

- **Urological surgeon:** A doctor who specialises in diseases of the urinary organs in females and the urinary tract and sex organs in males. Also called a urologist.

About the Author

Deb Fitzpatrick writes for adults, young adults and children. Her novels have been named Notable Books by the Children's Book Council of Australia, shortlisted in the West Australian Young Readers Book Awards, published in the US, and optioned for film. Deb lived in a shack in Costa Rica for four years where she became accustomed – well, almost – to orange-kneed tarantulas walking through her house, and sloths and spider-monkeys in the trees outside. Deb loves using stories from real life in her novels and regularly teaches creative writing to all ages. She has a Master of Arts from the University of Western Australia, and shares her life with a lovely family and their kelpie, who is absolutely not a failed sheep dog.

Acknowledgements

Huge thanks to Professor Ajay Rane OAM for entrusting me with the story of his life and that of his family. His generosity of spirit and abiding humility will be with me for years to come; several times Ajay expressed his disbelief that a book was being written about him, despite his lifetime of improving the lives of women and children worldwide. Ajay truly is a modern-day hero. I thank him also for his patience in dealing with my endless queries about his life and that of his parents and grandparents. Thank you, Ajay. I hope I have done your family's story justice.

Books can only happen with an amazing team working together to make it so. Thanks to Wild Dingo Press publisher, Catherine Lewis, for inviting me to write this book in the Aussie STEM Stars series and for offering me the particular gift of Ajay's story. Thank you to everyone at the WDP team for your work on this project.

I owe a huge debt of gratitude to Dianne Wolfer for so generously reading drafts and offering critical feedback and encouragement as I went. Thanks